20.21

HN100407

Kaleidoscope

Escape

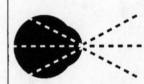

This Large Print Book carries the
Seal of Approval of N.A.V.H.

Kaleidoscope

Escape

Perspective Changes in a Suspense-Filled Romance

Kathleen Paul

Thorndike Press • Waterville, Maine

Published in 2005 by arrangement with Barbour Publishing, Inc.

Thorndike Press® Large Print Christian Romance.

The tree indicium is a trademark of Thorndike Press.

The text of this Large Print edition is unabridged. Other aspects of the book may vary from the original edition.

Set in 16 pt. Plantin by Ramona Watson.

Printed in the United States on permanent paper.

Library of Congress Cataloging-in-Publication Data

Paul, Kathleen.
    Escape / by Kathleen Paul.
      p. cm. — (Kaleidoscope ; bk. 4)
    "Thorndike Press large print Christian romance" — T.p. verso.
    ISBN 0-7862-7492-1 (lg. print : hc : alk. paper)
    1. Large type books.   I. Title.   II. Kaleidoscope (Thorndike Press) ; bk. 4.
    PS3566.A82627E83 2005
    813'.54—dc22   2005008763

To Richard V., who, through a myriad
of minor computer glitches and major
crashes, always managed to delve
into the memory of a confused PC
and find my manuscript.
And to his wife, Debby,
who had confidence in me that I could
finish this story and confidence that
Richard could find it one more time.
God bless good friends!

As the Founder/CEO of NAVH, the only national health agency solely devoted to those who, although not totally blind, have an eye disease which could lead to serious visual impairment, I am pleased to recognize Thorndike Press* as one of the leading publishers in the large print field.

Founded in 1954 in San Francisco to prepare large print textbooks for partially seeing children, NAVH became the pioneer and standard setting agency in the preparation of large type.

Today, those publishers who meet our standards carry the prestigious "Seal of Approval" indicating high quality large print. We are delighted that Thorndike Press is one of the publishers whose titles meet these standards. We are also pleased to recognize the significant contribution Thorndike Press is making in this important and growing field.

Lorraine H. Marchi, L.H.D.
Founder/CEO
NAVH

* Thorndike Press encompasses the following imprints: Thorndike, Wheeler, Walker and Large Print Press.

Chapter 1

The gate stood open. It was the delivery gate, less ornate than the heavy black iron grating in the front gate. Its locked bars usually served to keep the inmates in. Today it stood wide open.

A solemn young woman paused in her aimless walk across the expansive lawn. She stood rooted to the spot, staring at the open gate. A prayer formed in her mind, side by side with a wild hope. With deliberate nonchalance, she turned her head to survey the scene behind her. No one was close. The nearest attendant pushed old Mrs. Donaldson's wheelchair down the paved garden path on the other side of the rose hedge.

The girl's brown eyes scanned the windows of the mansion, an old plantation house, or rather, a replica of one. The Texas panhandle had not come by this impressive structure legitimately, for a Southern plantation was not in keeping with true Texas history. Instead, in the twenties, a businessman had built this extravagant layout.

The girl looked at its stately white columns lining the front verandah. No matter how elegant the house appeared, it was still a prison.

No one watched from the windows. No one on the immaculate lawn looked her way. She was just yards from the gate, the open gate.

With agonizing self-control, the slim figure strolled toward freedom. When the distance was but a few feet, she made a dash, rounded the corner, and dropped behind one of the brick pillars that held up the heavy iron gate. She was out.

Three years. She'd been inside for three years. Her heart pounded in her chest. Her thoughts jumbled with countless prayers. One surfaced above the others. She prayed for order. She must think clearly. She must be calm.

She knew exactly what she needed to do. She had planned her escape a thousand times. At the barred windows of her richly comfortable room, she had stared out over the wall. She had memorized the terrain beyond. Then, she had prayed for the opportunity. Now, prayers for strength and courage rose to her heavenly Father.

Every tree and bush to use as a screen was mapped out in her mind. Her goal was the riverbed. She had seen it from the elevated position of her window, though it was hidden from view now. No matter. She knew the way. She knew exactly what she would do. She had been planning and waiting and praying for two years. The first year didn't count. The first year was lost.

Her eyes darted down the dirt road and off to the highway. She was on the outside. The impossible had happened. "Nothing is impossible with God." Little did her captors know that over the past years, they had allowed her the one means to remain sane. She smiled cautiously with the knowledge that they had not been clever enough to keep the Bible out of her hands.

She must move. She had made the first step. She must not remain frozen. Three years, and she was out. If she was going to stay out, she must move.

She took a deep breath and ran the length of the wall to the place where she had planned to cross the road. With a quick look around to see if anyone was in sight, she crossed the highway and dropped behind a bush. With her eyes always on the next spot to hide, she crossed the field with amazing speed. Much sooner than seemed possible, she lowered herself over the embankment.

The riverbed was almost dry. A muddy stream coursed down the middle. She plucked off her shoes and stepped into the middle. The murky brown water was only ankle deep. She had expected it to be cool, but under the hot Texas sun, it had become tepid.

The riverbed cut deep into the land. When she stood, her head was well below the rim; she wouldn't be seen from a distance. She ran all out now, putting as much distance between herself and the last three years as she could. The trickling stream did little to impede her speed. The sandy bottom was hard enough to run on and smooth enough not to hurt her feet.

In her imagination, she had run like this. But in her daydreams, the atmosphere was sunny and bursting with life. Wildflowers, not the carefully cultivated blooms of the estate, but riotous wild blooms nodding their heads in the breeze, lined every path in her fantasy of escape. Birds rejoiced at her freedom with trilling spurts of song. That was fantasy and this was real. The day was gray and still.

She ran fast, heedless of the noise she made. She didn't fear detection. No one would overhear her splashing through the trickle of water, for she knew the area to be practically forsaken. She rarely even saw cattle out in this scrubby wasteland. Birds, jackrabbits, once a coyote, but never cows, horses, people. Beyond where the sprinklers gave life to the estate's lawns, the land was little more than a desert.

The heavy fall air stung her lungs as she gasped. The northern sky held dreary clouds. A low rumble of thunder drew her attention, and she paused for a moment with her hands on her knees, bent over to draw deep breaths into her aching lungs.

She heard no sound other than her own ragged breathing. Those clouds meant trouble. An unexpected gust of chilling wind foretold the coming cold. A Blue Norther it was called; she'd been imprisoned long enough in this area to recognize the signs.

She ran. She ran to get away. She ran until she couldn't, then she trudged along until she caught her breath and began to run again.

At first her prayers had surfaced merely in reiteration of all the last two years' prayers. The pleas were a litany born of desperate repetition. Soon, they simplified to the essential issues: "Lord, give me strength. Lord, protect me. Help me, Lord. Hide me. Don't let them find me." The water splashed warm against her legs, soaking the hem of her uniform's skirt.

Eventually, the stream widened and deepened. Small tributaries added to its strength. She looked again over her shoulder and supposed those heavy clouds were dumping water some miles away. The steep banks on either side of the creek began to worry her. She knew the water could rampage through these gullies with a force sufficient to carve away the heavy dirt. Was she safe? Would she hear a flash flood in time to scramble up the sides? Was the mental hospital far enough behind to chance walking in the open? "Oh God, guide me."

The stream became a lazy river. What river was this? How far did it go? In the three years that she had browsed through the extensive library at the hospital, she had never found a book containing maps of the area. No histories for the Texas panhandle to give her a clue. But she had a plan. Getting to the stream was only her first goal.

She slowed to a walk as the water rose above her knees, then edged over to the side, where it was ankle deep. Something moved in the water ahead, and she stopped to wait for it to pass. The stout body of a water snake glided lazily toward a patch of sun from a shady spot under a tree. His copper back bore wide, dark, ragged-edged crossbands. She held her breath, never taking her eyes off the snake until he was far enough away to be only a ripple in the water. Clouds gathered and less warmth radiated from the sun as it appeared and disappeared in a game of hide and seek.

The girl slipped from the water and collapsed under the tree, cold and shivering. Had the snake been a water moccasin? She didn't know one snake from another. She caught a sob as it rose to her throat, and she prayed she wouldn't fall apart. Three years of her life gone, and now she was out. She had to stay out. Clutching her shoes to her chest, she went back into the water.

Her mind pictured the activities on the estate. She had made her escape right after they had eaten lunch, so if she was lucky, they wouldn't notice she was missing until dinner. Would they use dogs to track her? Would they look for her at all? Of course, they would. They weren't paid to let her go. They were paid to keep her locked away.

She would not go back.

How long had she been out? She'd been in three years. Had she been out three hours?

It started to rain. *This is good after all,* she told herself. She was cold and wet, but the rain would shield her from curious eyes. She praised God for the rain even as she shivered. Perhaps the sheets of rain would obscure any footprints she'd left. Could dogs track in the rain? How long had she been out?

She came to a highway that crossed the river with a bridge. She sat under the bridge, out of the rain, resting. It was important to think clearly and stick to the plan. She had made the plan when she had plenty of time to weigh alternatives. Being wet and grimy might prove awkward. She'd have a hard time explaining what had happened.

She'd stick to her story as closely as she could, however. Her name was Daisy Madden. Daisy because of the beautiful wild appearance of the blossoms on the estate that contrasted with the otherwise pruned and cultivated gardens. The daisies had never seemed to fit into their surroundings, just as she had never fit. And "Madden" because she was mad to think she would ever escape. But she was out, and she was going to stay out.

The rain subsided. Daisy Madden climbed the embankment to the road and started another phase of her journey. Always with a prayer, she moved forward. Praying had become a habit. God was the only One with Whom she had felt comfortable talking during her years of captivity. She had no idea if she was going east, west, north, or south. She was just going, but God was going with her.

By now they had discovered she was gone. Would they call the police?

Daisy dodged to the side of the road every time she heard a car. The rain stopped, leaving the air wet and cold. The sun was down. This highway had few travelers.

She came to a rest stop beside the road. It had two picnic tables, a cement grill with rusted-out grating, and two terrible, smelly rest rooms. She ducked inside the door marked WOMEN to get out of the sharp wind. Exhausted, Daisy couldn't bring herself to sit on the cold, slimy floor. Fatigue compelled her to find some other shelter.

She slipped back outside and huddled behind the building out of the wind. She pulled the bulky sweater she wore close about her, covering more of the patient's uniform dress. The dress was a somber blue, like gray and blue that had been polished together. The resultant color made the cotton polyester material have a sheen to it. It was a simple shirtwaist, cut with a pocket on the bodice and in each side of the skirt. It didn't have a belt. Patients were not allowed to have belts.

Both the navy blue sweater and the dress were wet, but Daisy was beyond caring. Hunched against the cold concrete, she slowly slid to the ground. Her chin dropped to her chest. She fell into an exhausted sleep.

A noise woke her — but what? She stared into the darkness and thought she saw a movement. Some animal scurried between bushes, and she sighed her relief. Another noise beyond the building caught her ear. With cold and stiff muscles, she carefully crept to the corner. If she had to get up and run, they'd catch her.

Someone started whistling. The cheerful tune came clearly through the night air, and she peeked around the corner. A man crouched beside his car, changing a tire. He had a four-door sedan of a light shade; she couldn't tell what color in the dark of the night, for his car was at the edge of the pool of light coming from the top of one towering pole. The large man wore a heavy coat, wrapped warmly against the cold.

The thought crossed Daisy's mind that she had never been so cold. She shivered and her eye settled on the blanket he had thrown on the wet pavement to protect his clothing. Obviously it was an old, tattered thing. Surely he didn't value it.

He finished and threw the tools in the trunk, slamming the lid. The blanket still lay on the ground. He gathered something from the front seat of the car and carried it to the trash container. She heard him make some mild exclamation as he turned back to the car. He walked over and jerked up the blanket, then threw it in the backseat of the car.

His tall, solid form moved toward the building, and Daisy held her breath. He passed her and went to the opposite end, where he entered the door marked MEN.

She made a dash for the car and opened the back door. It was warm inside and smelled of tuna fish. Half a sandwich lay on the console between the two front seats. Without thinking, she reached out and took it. She was as hungry as she was cold. Her intention had been to snatch the blanket, but instead she unwrapped the sandwich and devoured it.

Whistling alerted her to the man's return. She'd been too slow, and now she had no shelter to hide her between the car and the building. Quickly, she got in and closed the door, but it didn't latch. She frantically scrunched down on the floorboard and drew the blanket over her.

The whistling stopped. What was he doing? The door to the back opened. She held her breath. She felt the blanket move around her ankles as he poked the end of the blanket in and slammed the door.

He hadn't seen her. He got in the car, turned the key in the ignition, and started down the road. At least he was going the right direction, away from the estate. He'd have to stop for gas or something, and she'd slip out.

She prayed. She had prayed at the estate to get out. She had prayed running in the river that she'd make it. She had prayed sitting under the bridge for a clear mind and protection. Now, she prayed this man was half-blind and perhaps a bit stupid.

He turned on the radio and switched through the stations until he found one he liked. He sang the music and crunched on something that was in a bag next to him. Once, he rolled down his window. Daisy guessed he was trying to stay awake, and she prayed he wouldn't fall asleep at the wheel. An accident was not part of her plans.

Chapter 2

A heavy hand dragged her back from a pleasant dream. She wanted to sleep. Persistent nudging against her shoulder would not go away. She shrugged and tried to burrow farther down into the covers. A voice called, "Hey, come on. Wake up."

She came awake all at once and struggled hopelessly to get out of the car. She was wedged in an awkward position between the seats, and the blanket had wrapped around her legs to further impede her.

"Take it easy." A pleasant voice. The man! She looked up into the face of the car's driver. He stooped beside the open back door so that his face was almost level with hers, the light in the car's ceiling illuminating his strong features. Green eyes flecked with brown looked darker than they really were. Dark brown hair curled thick and disorderly around his rugged face. Lines crossed his brow in furrows as a small smile tugged at the corners of his mouth. He looked puzzled.

He was seeing a remarkably disheveled young woman. She wore no makeup, but her dark frightened eyes, fringed with ample dark lashes, scarcely needed it. She was probably pretty, but her hair was wet and clinging to her muddied face.

"Let me help you get out." Without waiting for a response, he grabbed her below the arms and, with no apparent effort, pulled her up toward him. He didn't drag her out of the car, but allowed her to arrange herself in a more dignified position on the backseat.

"I gather I picked you up when I changed the tire." His tone was conversational.

She nodded her head.

"You ate the rest of my sandwich."

She nodded again. He seemed more amused than angry.

"I thought I must have thrown it away with the trash, but I could have sworn I left it in the car."

"I'm sorry," she managed to whisper.

"The lost sandwich doesn't matter." He grinned at her with a lopsided smile. "I was concerned I'd lost my mind. Then I began to hear noises in the backseat. I've been driving a long time, and I thought it was getting to me."

She looked down at her hands. Three years had passed since she had talked to anyone but an attendant or Dr. French. Should she tell him her made-up tale now or wait for questions? She decided to wait. She began to shiver.

"You're cold," he said. "Climb in the front seat, and we'll get moving again." He gave her his hand to get out and walked her around to the passenger door in front.

"You're soaked. Take the sweater off and put my coat on."

He proceeded to remove her sweater and throw it on the backseat. He wrapped his coat around her and pushed her into the car, then pulled the blanket out of the back to wrap around her legs and over her lap. Whistling, he returned to his side of the car, slammed the back door shut, got in, and started the car.

The warmth of his coat enveloped her, but instead of shivering less, she seemed to be shivering more.

"Why did you get in?" he asked.

"I was cold." Her voice sounded small and she couldn't hide the trembling.

"You sure are shivering. Maybe I should take you to a hospital. You may be suffering from exposure."

"No!" The word came out in a little gasp.

He studied her. She tried to look stony-faced, not revealing any emotion. The false mask accentuated her fear.

"Okay. No hospital." He saw her relax, but the shivering turned to shuddering. "You may be running a fever."

He reached out a hand, and she ducked.

"It's okay. I was only going to feel your forehead." Slowly this time, he reached out to touch the back of his fingers lightly to her forehead. "Well, I'm not much of a judge, but I don't think you have a temperature."

He paused and looked with unconcealed curiosity at his stowaway. "What's your name?"

"Daisy Madden."

"Hello." He extended a hand for a friendly handshake. "My name's Peter Hudson. I'm a rancher."

"You don't look like a rancher." She observed his college grad sweater and slacks.

"Well, Ma'am," he drawled, "seems I forgot my horse and Stetson back at the ranch."

She smiled at him, the first time she had smiled in a long time. Even the feel of it was strange to her face.

"What were you doing, soaked through and out in the middle of nowhere?"

He was direct, and she liked that. She was ready with her half-truth, half-lie story.

"I'm running away."

"What from and where to?"

"Where to doesn't matter." She purposely looked into his eyes, hoping to dispel any suspicion that her story was fabrication. "I have to find a job because I don't have any relatives to run to. What from is home. My mother is dead and my father drinks. Dad's not very pleasant when he drinks." She deliberately turned her head, staring out the side window, hoping to end the discussion. She'd decided over the two years of preparing her "history" that it was better to put forth an outline and let the listener fill in the details. She hadn't expected to feel like such a liar uttering the words out loud.

"The next town should pop up pretty soon. I'll have to stop and get gas." His voice was noncommittal. She had no way of knowing whether he believed her or not. The miles slipped away in silent darkness with only the radio commenting on the passage of time.

They pulled into an all-night convenience store. She would slip out here. She hadn't stopped shaking, though, and she wondered if something was wrong with her. He finished pumping the gas and stepped inside to pay. Now was her chance to find someplace to hide. Huge trash containers lurked behind the building. Beyond that, a parking lot sprawled around a shabby apartment complex.

He took longer than she expected, and still, she hadn't moved. She was out of her prison; if she blew it now, she'd have to go back. What would he do when he came back and found her gone? Would he look for her? Probably not. Would he call the police? She'd only stolen a sandwich. Maybe he was calling the police now. Not for the sandwich, but because she was a runaway.

She leaned forward and strained to peek around the pumps and inside the store. No, he was talking to the cashier. He was joking. She could see him laugh. If she could only stop shaking, she'd get out.

Too late. He pushed open the double glass doors and started toward the car. She'd have to make her escape at the next gas stop. She'd be warmer then, more rested. And there would be that many more miles between her and the estate.

As soon as he sat down behind the wheel, he handed her a warm sandwich and a cup of something hot.

"Put the hot chocolate down here until it cools a little. You'll scald your tongue. There's a special drink holder down here. See. The sandwich is just one of those microwave jobbies."

She had already unwrapped it.

"Slow down," he said, watching her first bites. "When you're that hungry you can get sick eating too fast."

She dutifully tried to eat more slowly, and he started the car again. When she was finished, she sipped on the chocolate. Finally, the shivering subsided.

"Thank you." She belatedly remembered her manners. He didn't answer, and she stole a look at him. He looked very serious as he gazed out at the road before them. Half asleep, she thought it was a shame that she had to slip away the next chance she got. He was not part of her plan. Now that she wasn't shivering anymore, though, she'd be able to think and make good her escape.

When she awoke, it was daylight. The car was stopped. The trunk slammed shut, and she twisted around to see Peter Hudson come around to her window. He opened the door.

"Good, you're awake. See if you can clean up your face a bit." He handed her one of those containers out of which you could pull a wet paper towel.

She scrubbed and looked up at him. He shook his head woefully.

"It's not going to work." He sounded disappointed. "You're still too messy to take in anywhere. People would notice you and wonder what happened, and that would make them remember you. I take it you'd rather not be noticed?"

It was a rhetorical question. He seemed to scarcely take note of her shaking head.

"Well, I had half a notion to drive straight through, but I'm more tired than I expected." He gazed off at the clouds, seemingly more concerned about the weather than his rider. "It still looks stormy and if I hole up for the day, it'll have a chance to clear.

"I'm going to get a motel room and get some shut-eye. You're welcome to take a shower and then do whatever you want. I'm not proposing anything indecent. I'm just going to sleep."

He saw the look of uncertainty on her face. She looked at him and she looked at her clothes.

"I'll never get a job looking like this." She wavered. "Are you sure?" She looked at him, wanting to trust.

He put his hand up in mock pledge. "You'll be as safe as my old maiden aunt."

"What's her name?" Daisy Madden asked.

He laughed. "You got me. I can't think of one." He turned serious. "It's all right, Daisy. You've had a rough deal and I'm not going to add to it."

His earnestness made her feel guilty, and she lowered her gaze from his honest eyes to stare at her hands.

"Okay," she said. *God, protect me,* she prayed.

Chapter 3

"You're a mess," Peter whistled in astonishment.

They were inside her motel room. He had gone into the office and secured two rooms while she waited in the car. He took some luggage in, and when the coast was clear, she got out and ran in. Rather, she started to run in, but she found that her legs had turned to spaghetti. If Peter had not been beside her, she would have hit the pavement. He swooped her into his arms and carried her across the threshold, put her on her feet, and quickly closed the door behind them.

"Are you sure I don't need to take you to a hospital?" She heard real concern in his voice and the sympathy nearly broke Daisy's resolve. His hands were on her elbows, supporting her, or she would have turned away.

Somehow his honest gaze made her feel more like a liar. Contemplating the lies as she plotted her escape was different from actually living the falsehoods.

"No," she said, unable to look him straight in the eye. "I'm all right."

"If he . . . hurt you just before you left, maybe a doctor should look at you."

Again, she felt the lump rise in her throat. She shook her head and took a deep breath, forcing herself to look up at him.

"It wasn't like that." Her voice broke under that steady look. Her eyes shifted away, and she tried again. "He . . ." She gave up and shrugged. One more lie wouldn't matter but still she could not utter it.

There was a moment's pause. His hands loosened their grip on her elbows, and since she didn't fall, he let go and stepped away from her.

He was still silent. She'd make one more try, as close to the truth as she could get. "I don't think the law can do anything to him for what he did. There's no proof."

Again, silence. She looked down at herself and had to agree she was a mess. Mud splattered her legs and dress. Scraggly hair hung around her thin shoulders. She looked in the mirror over the dresser and was feminine enough to be shocked. With no makeup and hair that had just grown with no trims, perms, or styling for three years, she looked bad. Add fatigue and fear and mud, and she looked horrible. Rather hopelessly, she began to pluck at the drying mud on her dress.

"We're going to have to do a complete overhaul," Peter acknowledged. "Here's some shampoo from my bag and a sweater that should swallow you up sufficiently. You go in the bathroom and hand out all your clothes. I'll take them to a Laundromat. Take a nice long bath or whatever, and crawl into bed when you get out. I'll lock the door and take the key."

"But you were going to sleep."

"I'm not the one who looks like the creature from the slimy lagoon or Swamp Man's sister."

His lack of gallantry comforted her and even brought a small smile tugging at the corner of her mouth. She followed his instructions.

He tiptoed in when he returned. His passenger was curled in the bed and never moved as he walked quietly around the room. Now he put the clothes on the end of her bed. He also placed a new toothbrush, a tube of toothpaste, a brush, and a comb there.

Peter Hudson stood staring at the girl

who called herself Daisy Madden. Was that much of her story true? He'd had three little sisters and had been in the habit of taking care of them. That was ancient history, though. Since then, he'd been to college and done a hitch in the Marines. He had, for all practical purposes, taken over running the family ranch. His sisters were grown and married. They no longer needed him to look after them, and he looked after cattle instead. He shook his head, bewildered by his own behavior of the past few hours. *Well, Lord,* he prayed, *it looks like I've picked up a stray. What am I going to do with her?*

Resigned to the fact that he was not going to get an immediate answer, he put himself to the tasks that would keep "the old horse ready." His mother had impressed upon him that his job was to be prepared for battle. Taking a moment to grab the Gideons' Bible and locate the verse, he looked at it with reassurance. The battle was the Lord's.

He put aside the problem of a frightened young lady under his protection. He wanted some sleep. He went to his own room and took a shower, but he dressed again before he lay down on the bed. He slept immediately.

A stealthy noise awoke him. He lay perfectly still for the minute it took him to orient himself then he got up and put his head out the door. The girl was fully dressed and tiptoeing away. That was the slight noise he had heard.

"You don't have to sneak out. You're free to go."

She jumped. "You were asleep."

"Have I done anything to make you treat me like the bogeyman?" His calm voice filled her again with guilt. Or maybe it just resurfaced. This lying wasn't as easy as she thought it would be. If only he weren't so nice.

"I'm sorry."

He held the door open with one hand and stepped back. After a moment, she went into his room.

Peter sat down on the edge of the bed.

"I was planning to eat dinner and then get back on the road. You're welcome to join me. I thought we'd talk a bit about finding you a job, Daisy."

She studied his face, but she saw nothing there but honesty. Maybe she could trust him a little, if she didn't forget to be careful. She nodded at him and was rewarded with a warm smile. He stood up and began gathering things together. Daisy just watched; she was wearing all her possessions.

The crowded restaurant was not conducive to a heart-to-heart chat. They didn't try. Peter watched her look at the menu, and then her eyes darted around the room. Was she wondering what to order? Maybe he should reassure her that he could afford anything she might want. He ordered for both of them, but he decided the menu wasn't the problem when she still showed signs of nervousness after the waitress had gone off with their order.

"What's wrong? Are you afraid you'll get spotted? I'll bet we're two hundred and fifty miles from where we joined courses."

Daisy gave him a quick, unsteady smile. "I haven't been around people much lately. I'd forgotten what it felt like to be in a crowd."

A question sprang to his lips and he suppressed it. He knew from his experience raising sisters that the best confidant asked few questions.

When the meal came, she bowed her head for a moment. In a quick, silent prayer, she thanked God for protecting her and giving her unexpected help. She asked for blessings upon Peter Hudson for his generous spirit. Raising her head, she caught him watching her.

"You were praying?"

"Yes," she answered.

Again, he looked bewildered. "Daisy, you are the most peculiar runaway I've ever heard of."

Confused by the remark, she chose to ignore it and concentrated on the food before her. She found that she was starving. Nothing inside had ever tasted as fine as the things she had eaten on the outside, even though the menus at the estate were always a fine bill of fare. Daisy cleaned up every morsel on her plate and sighed with contentment.

As she looked across the table at her companion, she noticed that Peter was only halfway through his meal. She must have wolfed down her food. A blush stained her cheeks. Her three years inside the hospital had apparently washed away good manners. She ducked her head, hoping to avoid the penetrating observation of her rescuer. Peter noticed.

"Didn't that drunken father ever feed you?" he asked, a smile hovering around the corners of his mouth. Daisy glanced up to see the humor with which he viewed her distress. She blushed a deeper red. She wanted desperately to have him as a friend, but she'd started by lying to him, and she had to ditch him as soon as possible. He was not a part of her plan! She couldn't afford a friend.

"Do you want another roll?" He offered her the basket.

Now she had the impression he was teasing her. In her strange upbringing, there had never been anyone to tease her in this gentle, brotherly way. She wasn't quite sure what he was up to.

"If you'll wait a minute until I catch up, I'll order us some pie with ice cream."

Was it the mention of the pie on top of everything else? Or was it the chaotic atmosphere of the restaurant that suddenly seemed to swell in her ears with its noise and push in all around her? Was she somehow sick from the exposure or the fear? She only knew her head was swimming.

"What's wrong?" His voice was sharp.

"I feel faint. No," she said as a new sensation flooded through her, "I'm going to throw up."

He was curt. "The rest room's by the door we came in, behind the register. Move." His military command underlined the words.

He sat quietly, watching her push through the crowd, praying she'd make it. When she was out of sight, he returned to the few bites left of his dinner.

Shaking his head, he wondered what he was going to do with the little heifer. One of his sisters might befriend her. That would be an option he would put to her. They each lived in larger towns where she could possibly get a job. He wondered off-hand what she could do. So far he knew she could sleep and eat — and she might have just flunked eating.

Another thought occurred to him that made his brows draw together in a sharp frown. It was time they did some real talking. A few minutes after he'd finished, Daisy returned. She was pale, but no longer green.

"I suppose you'll be hungry again in a hundred miles." He rose to greet her and grabbed the check. He looked up to see her swaying and grabbed her around the waist. "Come on, Puny. We'll stick you in the backseat of the car. You can lie down and close your eyes."

They drove a hundred miles while the night blackened the surrounding country-side. Here and there lights glowed, indicating the presence of houses and farms.

Peter's thoughts drifted through a series of business affairs and the order and manner that must be used to deal with them. Persistently, the stray thought of the homeless waif in the backseat interrupted his tidy business dealings.

Where had she been that she was no longer used to crowds and wore dresses that looked like institutional issue? She certainly had not been treated kindly. Was the exhaustion physical, emotional, or both?

He heard a movement, and then he felt her warm breath on his cheek. She was peeking over his shoulder.

"I feel better now. May I sit in the front seat?"

He pulled the car over to the side of the road, and she hopped out of the backseat, opened the door to the front, and slid in beside him. He reached over the back of the seat and pulled the blanket to the front, draping it over her legs.

He turned off the engine, and her head came up quickly. He saw her startled eyes searching the darkness, trying to see his face. The light came from a highway lamp behind him. He could see the concern and fear flicker in her eyes.

"Don't be so afraid. I just want to talk to

you." Peter cleared his throat. Whatever had scared this child had scared her through and through. He looked out into the night. It was a lonely stretch of road. The stupid kid could be out here with a mad rapist. Thank God their paths had crossed. He proceeded carefully. "I want you to trust me. I want to help you, but I can only do that if you're truthful."

Involuntarily, not realizing how much she gave away by the gesture, Daisy winced and abruptly turned away.

"Daisy, are you pregnant?" He put the question to her bluntly.

Her gaze came back to his face, a genuine smile on her lips. Her eyes danced merrily as she shook her head vigorously. "No."

"Why is that amusing?" Given the circumstances, the question was legitimate. She was running away. Physically, she was tired beyond what would be considered normal. And she was experiencing nausea.

Peter watched her carefully, hoping to gain more information from her expressions and movements than from her words. Obviously, she would willingly disclose only so much.

"I can't be pregnant. I wasn't allowed to date." Her voice cut off abruptly. The smile vanished and she again preferred to look out the window rather than at her inquisitor. She did not see the look of exasperation pass over his features.

"What kind of work are you going to do?"

"Waitress."

"All right, when we get to Dooley, I'll introduce you to the right people."

"Where's Dooley?"

"It's a small south Texas town. I was raised there, and I know most everybody. Or I've got sisters in Corpus Christi, Victoria, and Houston. I'm sure one of them would take you in and help you get started."

"No." She whispered the word, but it sounded definite. "I have a plan. I must stick to my plan. It's already been muddled some, and if I get too far from it, I'll . . . mess up. I can't afford to mess up."

Daisy turned pleading eyes to his darkened form. She could not see his face, could not read his reaction. She reached out and clutched his arm. "Please," she said, her voice trembling.

He laid a strong hand across hers and discovered hers shaking. *God,* he prayed, *what is the right thing to do for this girl?*

Chapter 4

A car pulled to a stop behind them, and its headlights filled Peter's car with light. Peter twisted around to look.

"It's the state patrol. Don't lose your head. He probably just wants to know if we've got car trouble."

"Do we?"

"No, stick to the truth. You've been nauseated. We stopped for awhile."

"That's not all true," she objected. "We didn't stop because I was sick."

"I must say I'm surprised to hear you objecting to such a little prevarication." Peter chuckled. "It's true enough." He turned his head and rolled down the window as he greeted the officer.

So, thought Daisy, *he isn't as stupid as I had prayed for. He knows I'm hiding at least part of the truth.* She had no more time to think over his statement.

"You folks having trouble?" The patrolman's tone was friendly as he briefly shone his flashlight in their faces.

Peter answered, nodding toward his passenger. "She gets carsick. We just stopped to rest a little."

The officer interrupted. "It's not exactly safe to sit on the highway at night. There's an all-night diner about twelve miles down the road. Perhaps your Mrs. could get a soft drink to settle her stomach."

"Thanks, Officer." Peter began rolling up the window and the uniformed man walked away.

Peter turned on the engine and directed the car out onto the road.

"How old are you?" he asked.

"Twenty-one."

He let out a muffled whistle.

"That officer has better perception than I do. I thought you were about sixteen. I was going to pass you off as my daughter."

"You're not that old," she protested.

"I'm twenty-nine, and I was going to glower to put a few extra years on my countenance."

Her ripple of laughter touched his heart. This child was made to laugh, and someone had stripped all the joy from her life, crushing her spirit. Well, if they wanted to get to her again, they'd have to go through him.

He didn't stop to think about it, but his protective feelings were not quite the same as the brotherly surveillance he'd kept on his sisters. Somehow, knowing her true age had changed something. Unconsciously, he forgot about getting this child under some protective custody, some organization that dealt with abused children.

After a few miles of silence, Peter flicked on the radio and searched for some music. He zeroed in on a station and let it play. After several songs, Daisy spoke up.

"Last night you sang along."

"I didn't know I had an audience." Peter laughed. "If I remember, I was singing loudly to help keep myself awake."

They listened without comment for awhile.

"Tell me about your sisters," Daisy requested.

Peter gladly jumped on the topic. Since Daisy wasn't going to go back to sleep, maybe she would reveal a little more of her background through conversation.

"My sisters are all younger than I am. The youngest is Midge — or Margaret. She's the brainy one. She's in Houston with her husband, Mike. Mike is a computer processor instructor at the university, and Midge is studying law. We have an uncle on my father's side who is a lawyer.

"The middle sister is Scram. Her real

name is Sarah. Sarah is twenty-five and lives in Victoria with her engineering husband, Joe. They have two kids, Tiger and Tabitha. Tiger is three and Tabitha is five.

"Lisa is twenty-seven, married to a teacher. She works in the museum in Corpus Christi part-time. They have no children, but they are trying to adopt."

"Do you like having a family?"

"Yes, don't you?"

"I haven't got any."

"How about your drunken father?"

Quietly, she said, "Would you count a drunken father as family?"

Peter could see the logic in this. He didn't contest the point.

"You haven't any sisters or brothers?"

"I have an uncle, but I'm not much use to him. I haven't seen him in three years, and he made it very plain when we parted that he would like to never see me again."

"Is this your father's brother? They sound like they are cut out of the same cloth."

Peter wondered what sort of callous cad could turn his back on Daisy. He'd met many families where the familial characteristics were not a Roman nose and wide-set eyes, but a nasty temper and sharp sarcastic tongues. If Daisy was raised in an environment of selfishness and abuse, why did she seem so utterly defenseless and pure? And where had she been brushed with religion? Not many people prayed over their food in a restaurant.

"Yes," she answered Peter's question. "But I've never been around him much."

Memories flooded through her mind. She was little Julie again, laughing as she raced with her carefree daddy across the lawn of their farmhouse home. The impressive old home had been purchased by her dad for her mom as a wedding present. Together they had completely renovated and furnished it with the exquisite taste and lavishness that much money allows. Antiques crowded each room. Handcrafted decorations that her mother had ferreted out of bazaars and craft shows all over the country covered the walls and tables.

A swimming pool and a stable graced the back acreage. Her daddy had taught her to swim and ride almost before she was walking. Julie spent hours of almost every day in her father's company. His fortune had been passed down through several generations, growing with each succession. Her father's business philosophy was to keep in touch and in control, but hire someone else to do the work.

Julie's fondest memories, and the most tragic, were associated with the fun shopping trips to country fairs and bazaars, rummaging around antique stores. She and her mother would take off in a fancy red pickup and "scrounge," as her mother called it, in every old furniture store they could find. Or they'd fly to some special event such as a state craft show. Sometimes her daddy would come along, and then the trip was more fun. Worn out from spending money, Mom would rest in the hotel, and Julie and her daddy would explore whatever town they were in.

When she was eight, they had planned a minor excursion to visit a craft show in Iowa. They were going in a friend's small private plane. Julie, however, came down with a bad cold and an ear infection, and she was left at home with the housekeeper. The plane crashed, and Julie was a very rich and lonely orphan.

Uncle Jacob swooped into her life.

Uncle Jacob was the opposite of his brother, her father. He inherited all the lust for power, the drive to achieve that had benefited the fortunes of the family ancestors. He scorned his older brother's lifestyle and resented the disinterested brother who controlled the interests of the family business. With great relish, Uncle Jacob took over. His joy was hampered by the presence of a sprightly heiress-in-waiting, Julie Jones.

He developed a plan of action. For years Julie attended fine boarding schools all over Europe. She never stayed long at any one because she was "to have a taste of many different cultures." As a result, she never formed any deep and lasting friendships that would complicate things for the uncle whose main interest was his own profit.

Uncle Jacob handled vacations and holidays much the same way. He hired different companions to escort her as she traveled. She never had the same one twice, and they were carefully selected to discourage comradeship. Julie was never allowed to visit a school chum's home during the school breaks but was trudged off to more exposure to culture under a carefully screened dour dame's unfriendly escort.

Fortunately, one of these caretakers was Frances Belvedere, a religious fanatic. Mrs. Belvedere's creed didn't impress Julie, but during the course of their summer together, the older woman hauled Julie to evangelistic meetings in various countries. Memories of sitting in her mother's lap and hearing Bible stories resurfaced. Julie remembered the contentment associated with these cozy times. The message of hope reached her, and she easily gave over a life of despair to the One Who saves.

"You've been quiet a long time." Peter interrupted her memories. "I thought you'd gone to sleep again."

She shook her head.

"Would you like to drive? I could use a break."

She shook her head again. "I don't have a license."

She'd been welcomed "home" when she was eighteen with the gift of a beautiful, sleek little red sports car. She had not seen her uncle in years; he had only sent her short business letters, telling her where she was going, what she would be doing, and who was coming to do it with her. Consequently, she felt no affection for her uncle. She met her aunt for the first time and immediately felt sorry for her. Maria Jones clearly feared her husband.

Two weeks later, Julie knew the woman had good reason to be afraid of this man. Kind Uncle Jacob who smiled with his lips but never with his hard, cold eyes, slipped Julie a drug that knocked her out. Uncle Jacob then secreted his niece away to Dr. French's estate, where she was to undergo an unneeded recovery program for drug abuse. The charlatan doctor got a handsome recompense for keeping her drugged for six months. By then, a very confused Julie was physically ill.

For six months after that, she had daily sessions with Dr. French in which she tried to tell him the truth. One day she realized he knew the truth and was paid well not to help her. Since Dr. French wasn't interested in losing a high-paying patient, she tried talking to the attendants and finding one who would help her. They were used to crazy talk from the patients. After all, wasn't this where the extremely rich sent their mentally unbalanced?

Quite abruptly, she gave in. All outward appearances indicated she had resigned herself to her fate. She continued to see Dr. French for an hour of "therapy" three mornings a week. He sat and read, or he did paperwork (a crossword puzzle) or sometimes played solitaire. Occasionally, he'd notice her and say, "Miss Jones, anytime you feel like it, we'll discuss your problems." She never felt like it.

At first she was bent on revenge. Her uncle had done this to have control over the inheritance. She would get out and prove she was healthy and of a sound mind. As her thinking cooled down and became more rational, she could see the things he had done over the years to make sure no one knew her well, so no one would come to her aid. He had reckoned without God, though. God, her powerful ally, would have to be given full reign to make right the horrible wrong. Her dilemma was beyond the powers of any human she could call on.

At first she had hoped that something would come to the notice of the authorities, and her situation would be rectified. State health inspectors came and went, though, and no irregularities came to light.

As the months passed, gaining freedom became more important than seeking revenge. To say she could bring about justice was pointless.

If she got out, she realized, she would concentrate only on staying out. If she fought her powerful uncle, he would know where she was and throw her back in the estate. If she continued to be a problem, she had no doubt that Julie Jones would unfortunately succeed in a suicide attempt.

She decided that she would turn justice over to God and take care of living on her own.

Planning a new life was her best option. She'd already seen half the world, and her curiosity over what living a normal life would be like was intense. She had never been grocery shopping, for instance, or made her own dentist appointment. She began to like the idea of shedding the person of Julie Jones and becoming someone who mopped floors and shopped for bargains.

Time passed within the confines of the French Estate Private Hospital. Julie Jones became a model resident, quiet, not demanding, never bothersome.

Chapter 5

Peter sang quite vigorously with the radio. Daisy reluctantly opened her eyes and became aware of her surroundings. The road stretched before them and disappeared into darkness.

"Where are we?" she asked.

"South of San Antonio," Peter answered cheerfully. "We'll get to Dooley in the morning, probably around nine o'clock. But, I've got to get some coffee and my dinner is all gone. Are you in the least bit hungry?"

In fact, she was once again starving, but she answered demurely, "I am."

"I'm trying to remember what's along this road that might be open all night. That is, something other than a beer hall. Keep your eyes open for a truck stop."

Two hours later, they came to something Peter thought was suitable. Meanwhile, he had bought them chips and soda when he stopped for gas. Daisy had drifted off to sleep again.

Peter parked the car outside the diner,

thinking he'd get out and stroll around in the cold air before waking Daisy. He gazed at his sleeping rider and gently pushed back a lock of hair that had fallen across her face. Suddenly he withdrew his hand. He had not liked the sensation that had flashed through him. Her eyelashes were too long, and he knew they covered eyes that were too innocent for their own good. Her tiny nose was no longer red from cold and crying. Her lips were tender and pink.

She was not strikingly beautiful, but her sweetness attracted him. This would not do. Taking care of a girl like he would one of his sisters was one thing. Getting romantic and sentimental was another.

He cleared his throat gruffly and put a firm hand on her shoulder. "Let's eat." He promptly got out of the car.

She was getting out of her door rather slowly, not quite awake.

"Lock your side, Daisy." He glanced up to see if she had heard him. Two police came out of the restaurant door. One was chewing absently on a toothpick until he turned and caught sight of Peter and Daisy. His attention was arrested and he seemed to be weighing something in his mind.

Peter felt a stab of uneasiness. He

quickly came around the front of the car and impatiently locked the door for Daisy, then shut it with a thud.

He whispered, "Fight with me, Daisy." He answered the questioning look she threw him. "There are policemen just a few feet behind you."

She jumped in without losing a second to thinking. "Why are you so grumpy? I'm not the one who decided to drive all night."

"I'm grumpy because I don't like visiting your relatives, and if we drive all night, I can sleep through one whole day of the abominable visit."

"I don't make such a fuss when we visit your folks."

"My folks don't serve a noodle casserole at every meal and listen to twangy country music at full volume twenty-four hours a day," Peter complained bitterly.

He took hold of her arm and started toward the restaurant door, staying between her and the officers as they passed. He hoped the men hadn't gotten a good look at her in the shadowy light. He also hoped he and Daisy sounded natural in their roles as a bickering couple.

When they got inside, he told her to go to the rest room immediately and stay five minutes. He didn't want them to get a better look at her in the bright fluorescent lighting.

He took a booth in the almost-empty diner and ordered for both of them. Peter sighed his relief as the policemen got in their black-and-white car. He froze as he watched an officer talk for a minute on his car radio.

Finally they rolled out. They hadn't looked too anxious to catch any desperate criminals. Man, he was getting nervous. How much of what Daisy had told him was true? He guessed about half. Now he wondered which half was true? And what was the real story to fill in the false half?

The waitress brought his cup of coffee, saying something about the weather and the pain of being up when normal people were in bed. He responded as he should, but he felt a growing uneasiness. Nervously, he kept checking the door marked WOMEN at the end of the room, waiting for it to open.

The waitress returned with the two plates.

"Would you mind checking the ladies' room for me? My wife has been ill, and she's taking a long time."

"Sure thing. What's her name?" The

waitress glanced toward the closed door.

"Daisy," he answered.

He watched as she went down the length of the room. Suppose the little idiot had slipped out, thinking she would make it on her own? He held his breath as the waitress disappeared. Immediately, the door re-opened, and she came out, looked at him with a frown, and shook her head. Peter jumped up and started for the door.

"Maybe she went to the car," he threw over his shoulder.

Outside he looked around. He knew she wouldn't be in the car, but he looked anyway. He walked quickly to the back of the building. Where would she go?

If I were foolish and scared, without an ounce of sense, where would I run to? he asked himself.

He surveyed the area. *I'd head for town to get a job as a waitress.* He took giant strides toward the lights of the small sleeping town. *Now, where would I hide until morning?*

About half a mile down the road was a school bus shelter. *Dear God, let the little idiot be there.*

She was. She heard him coming and nearly died before she realized it was him. When she saw his familiar frame in the doorway of the shelter, she leaped up and grabbed him, burying her face in his coat. His arms came around her, and he rocked her comfortingly back and forth. She cried softly.

"Come on, pull yourself together. They've gone, and they weren't the least bit interested in us."

She sniffed loudly and he pulled a handkerchief out of his pocket. She blew her nose.

"Now, you're going to have red, puffy eyes again," he chided her. "I told the waitress you'd been ill, so she'll just think you're having a bad time of it. Let's go back before you get too cold."

They walked back to the truck stop. He kept his arm around her shoulders, saying nothing.

The waitress greeted them with concern. "Are you okay, Honey?"

Daisy managed to nod.

"She wanted some fresh night air. Now, let's see if we can persuade her to eat a little."

"That's the right idea. I'll get your plates. I put them back in the kitchen to keep them warm."

She bustled away, and Peter leaned over to whisper in Daisy's ear, "For Pete's sake,

56

eat like you're sick, not like a wolfhound."

She grinned up at him. "Can we take a doggie bag?"

"Yes, and I'll buy you breakfast by the gulf in Corpus Christi if you'll behave yourself for what's left of tonight."

Chapter 6

They reached Corpus Christi at seven in the morning and ate in a little café next to the beach.

Peter smiled at her. "I thought I'd picked up a truck driver by the way you've been eating." His good-natured teasing brought a smile to her lips. "Do you feel as tired as you were?"

"No, much better," she answered.

"Good. Your body is at least recovering from your ordeal. Now, tell me how you are doing otherwise."

"What do you mean?"

"Emotionally?"

"I'm okay. I know I've just got to do what's got to be done. I'm not so panicky feeling."

"Spiritually?"

"I trust God. He got me out of there. It took three years, but if I'd left a day before, I wouldn't have had you to help me." She smiled at him shyly. "Thank you. You really did rescue me."

"Bring on the dragons, fair lady. I

haven't had so much fun since Scram accidentally sold Dad's prize stallion at an auction for fifty bucks, and I had to get him back before Dad found out."

"Did you do it?"

"Yes, Ma'am," he drawled, grinning at her.

"It would be so wonderful to have family. I'm going to get married and have lots of children so they can play with each other and not be lonely and always have each other to run to." She was staring out at the gulf. Peter thought she didn't even realize she had expressed her dream out loud.

"We're going to be later than I thought getting to Dooley. Come on."

Daisy hesitated.

"Maybe I shouldn't go with you to Dooley."

Peter held his breath. He had feared they would have to cross this bridge. He had prepared some mighty good arguments.

"You see," she continued, "my plan is that at every place I stop, nobody from where I was will know where I've gone. That way I won't be linked from one place to the next. I'll change my name and work at a different occupation so they won't always look for a waitress."

"Daisy, even if your drunken father files a missing person report, you're twenty-one; you don't have to go back to him."

Daisy stared down at her empty plate. This was going to be hard. She had thought that the lies she had practiced would flow from her mouth. The last thing she wanted to do was lie again to Peter. The glib tales stuck in her throat.

"You don't know him," she said simply.

"If you tell the law your reason for being afraid, they will protect you."

"Forever, Peter? They can't watch one person forever, and he would wait."

Her eyes met his, and he saw the fear there.

"Come on," he said abruptly. He stood up and reached for her arm. "We'll talk in the car."

They were five miles out of town before he spoke again.

"Daisy, I just can't let you go off by yourself. You come to Dooley and get a job, and I can keep my eye on you. Wouldn't you like to know there is someone to come to if your father shows up?"

"Yes," she answered truthfully. The prospect of facing Uncle Jacob, or even Dr. French, left her breathless.

"I'll pretend I don't even know you, so

no one will know that I brought you to town, and no one will know where you came from."

"Just for a little while," she conceded and did not notice the slow smile that spread across Peter's face. "My plan is to only stay two or three months in one place."

"Are you going to do that for the rest of your life?"

"No, just until I change enough. I have to gain weight and change the color of my hair. And, I have to figure out what kind of clothes I'm going to wear. Before I would have picked soft pastel colors. I like ruffles and lace. But I thought I'd try bold colors now. And, when I change my hair color, that will affect the colors I should wear."

Peter grinned. There were times when Daisy could have been voicing the thoughts of any of his three sisters, except he never heard one of them wanting to gain weight.

"It seems like you're going to a lot of trouble. If there is a description of you, the police will only be interested for a few weeks," Peter pointed out. "Then their minds will be filled with the latest happenings, and you'll be history."

"He'll send out a private detective,

maybe a lot of them. And there might be a reward."

Peter raised his eyebrows.

"He's got a lot of money," she explained, not mentioning that a great deal of it was really hers.

"Daisy, did you take anything with you when you left? Something that he could claim you stole?"

"No, I didn't take anything."

"Then I still say you are safe. He can't kidnap you."

Silence met his proclamation. He looked over at her. She stared out the front window, and he could only see her profile. Clearly, kidnapping was exactly what she thought her drunken father would do.

In his dealings with his sisters, he had learned some procedures that guaranteed cooperation. He decided to call upon his old expertise.

"Well, we'll stop at the next town, and I'll get you the hair dye. What color do you want?"

She turned unbelieving eyes to him.

He continued, "I'd better get a scarf to cover your head until you've had a chance to dye it. I can't think how we could get it dyed before we get there. It's a shame we didn't think of it while we were in the motel."

"Thank you," she whispered, her eyes still filled with disbelief.

"You just remember to get in touch with me if you're in trouble. I'll give you several numbers where you can reach me or leave a message." He took a hand off the steering wheel and covered one of hers, giving it a squeeze. "Promise?"

"I promise."

"And, you won't take off without telling me good-bye, no matter what?"

She didn't respond, and he squeezed her hand again. "Promise?" he demanded.

"I promise."

"Good. There's a drugstore up here in the next town that should be open."

They parked about a mile outside of Dooley.

"Now when you get to town, go to Rio Street. It'll be right after the bank. Turn left and go to the third block. There's a big white house on the corner. That's the McKays'. They have two pieces of rental property behind their place, and the little servants' quarters house has been for rent since the beginning of summer. If that rented while I was out of town, Mrs. McKay will help you find a place.

"Go there first and dye your hair. Put

on that new dress and get out and find a job."

He reached in his rear pant pocket to pull out his wallet. He took three one-hundred-dollar bills out of it and handed them to Daisy. She gasped.

"I don't like traveler's checks," he explained.

"I can't take this," Daisy objected.

"It's already in your hand, and I'm not taking it back. We'll call it a loan. If you don't get a chance to pay it back to me, you can give it to someone in trouble years from now, and we'll consider it even."

"You've been so good to me. I've thanked God a hundred times for you."

"We sit here much longer and it'll blow the whole thing. Someone will drive by and recognize my car. Now, hop out."

She did and got the suitcase out of the back. Peter had explained to her that she had to have luggage and a purse to avoid suspicion. The suitcase only had one dress in it. He had bought it and brought it back to the car with the suitcase, purse, and hair dye. He instructed her to buy more clothes in Dooley, and he told her the two cheapest stores to go to.

"Wait," he called just as she turned to

leave. "Tuck your hair in the front. It's showing again."

She obeyed.

"See you later, Daisy."

"Remember, you don't know me," she warned.

"I'll remember." He turned the key in the ignition and left her trudging down the road. He glanced in the rearview mirror. Not know her? He'd never be able to forget her.

Chapter 7

Peter Hudson warded off the enthusiastic greeting of his hound, Sidney, and went straight to the phone. The dog persisted in demanding a proper greeting, and Peter's vague words and absentminded pats did little to satisfy him. Sidney sat at Peter's feet as he perched on the edge of his desk and fumbled through a rolling address gadget. It took him a minute to find the Dallas number he wanted. Impatiently, he dialed it and fumed when he had to leave a message to have the call returned.

Sidney sighed heavily, and Peter looked down at his faithful and momentarily disgruntled companion. Disappointment dragged at the basset's already woebegone expression. Mournful eyes gazed up at him, and the long droopy ears limply hung beside the melancholy expression. The fleeting joy of greeting, the exuberance of his welcome were past. Old Sidney was now in his regular hangdog mode. Peter slipped into his leather chair and reached down to caress the dog's ears and neck with the proper affection due to man's best friend.

"Old boy," commented Peter, "I've got a problem and the problem is female. And the female has a problem."

Sidney leaned into the massaging hand and offered a deep-throated rumble that sounded very much like sympathy.

"Our uncomplicated bachelor life may undergo some severe trials."

Mail had piled up on Peter's desk, and he sorted through it, finding it hard to keep his mind on the mundane business. In an effort to get his mind off the multitude of questions, he called his office to get a rundown from his secretary on what had transpired since she contacted him the day he left Denver.

"It sure took you a long time to get home, Mr. Hudson," Mrs. Wilson complained. "If you hadn't shown up today, I was going to contact the state troopers to look for you."

"That would have complicated matters," he said under his breath.

"Pardon?" said Mrs. Wilson.

"Oh, nothing. I just ran into some hitches." Was Daisy technically a hitchhiker or a stowaway? Was one land and one water? Or was it determined by how you got on board?

"Mr. Hudson, I asked you if you had car trouble." Mrs. Wilson's querulous voice came over the line.

"No, just a flat tire. But things like that can lead to complications." He smiled, then decided to leave the subject. "Come by the house on your way to lunch and pick up these papers from Denver to type. You can bring me the Henderson deal to look over."

"Yes, Sir."

As soon as he hung up, Peter knew he was still at the mercy of his chaotic thoughts. He sat back in his leather desk chair and stared for a moment at the ceiling. He had only one recourse under the circumstances. If he could not control his thinking, he'd better turn it over to Someone more capable. He grinned as he bowed his head to submit his will to his Maker and ask for guidance.

The expected phone call finally came.

"Hello, Uncle Henry, I'm in need of your help."

"Sure, Peter, anything I can do."

"I want someone investigated, and I want it done quietly."

"This sounds very interesting, Peter. You don't usually get involved in this sort of thing. Do you suspect one of your business contacts has gotten into something shady?"

"No, Uncle Henry. I've fallen in love, and I think the girl is in big trouble, but I can't get her to tell me everything yet."

There was dead silence on the other end. Peter waited. Finally, his uncle's calm Texas drawl came back on the line.

"You better give me some details, Son. We'll see what we can do."

"I can't tell you her name. I'm pretty sure she lied to me about that. I picked her up in the panhandle about twenty miles north of Dalhart, on Highway 385. She was at a rest stop there. She was wearing a dress that looks like she'd been in some kind of institution, a uniform of some sort. Good quality, not what you would expect from a prison. And she's too old to have been in a private school, although that was the quality of the dress. It had a name stamped on the inside collar, but it was blurred. The middle word was Estate with a capital 'E.' The first word started with 'Fr' and had four more letters I couldn't make out. The next two words were a disaster. I couldn't make out the third one, and as to the last word, I'd guess eight or nine letters and the last one looked like an 'l,' or the number one."

"Okay, I've got that down. Now, are you going to satisfy your favorite uncle's curiosity?"

Peter complied, telling all, even to the point of the moment when he knew he loved her, in the school bus shelter.

"Uncle Henry, she is a naïve idiot. If someone doesn't take care of her, I swear the big bad wolf will come out of the woods and carry her off."

"But why do you have to be the one to protect her?"

"Because I've gone swimming in those big, sad eyes," Peter answered matter-of-factly. "If I'm wrong about her, I'll eat my hat and pull myself together. I don't intend to be made a chump of by a pretty little thing who's got a real good act." Peter paused, contemplating his own words. "I can't convince myself that she's not on the level, and I'm willing to go out on a limb to find out. See what you can find out on solid ground, and be ready to throw me the lifeline if I fall out of the tree into a lake of lament." His voice had lightened as he expressed his serious feelings under the guise of humor.

"Okay, Son," answered the lawyer. "I'm convinced you've got it bad when you start spouting bad poetic dribble. You've always been a sensible fellow. I don't know many young scalawags who manage to lose their hearts and keep their heads. I'll put a private detective who is very discreet on this one and call as soon as I have news." Peter heard the old man sigh. "I guess I just have to say it, even though your words sound like you're standing firm. Pray this one through, Peter. Don't leave God out of this most important decision of your life. We both know how many miserable unions there are out there. Love and marriage are more crucial than any executive decision you'll ever make in your entire illustrious business career."

"I know, Uncle Henry," Peter agreed with a wry grin. "Your sermon also reminds me that I have other people who care enough about me to be praying I make the right moves."

"You're right there, Boy. You know I'll share all this with your beautiful aunt."

"I didn't think you'd even try to keep it from your wife. That would be impossible — and we leave the impossible to God, right?"

"Right." His uncle's rich chuckle came over the line.

Peter hung up feeling relieved. He wondered how long the investigation would take. He wondered how Daisy looked in her dark auburn hair. Had she found a job? Did she go shopping for bold colors or pastels? What was she going to eat for dinner? Did that little servants' quarters come with pots and pans? What if she skipped town on him? He knew the answer to that one. He grinned. He'd be sending out more private detectives to track down one idiotic waif.

Chapter 8

Finding the McKay residence was no problem. But Mrs. McKay was the mothering sort, and she wanted very much to take this shy young thing under her wing. She would have liked to know all of Daisy's troubles.

Daisy merely said, "I was unhappy at home, so I ran away. I want to find a job and be my own boss."

Mrs. McKay nodded wisely. "There's a position open at the café."

"A waitress?" Daisy could not believe her good fortune.

"Yes. Do you have experience?"

Daisy's face fell. "No, none."

"Well, you go down and ask anyway." Mrs. McKay gave her an encouraging pat on the shoulder.

Daisy let Mrs. McKay's pleasant voice wash over her as she turned her attention to the servants' quarters. The small white house looked like an elaborate playhouse built for a rich child. There were two rooms, the bathroom and the front room.

The bathroom had a shower and no tub. This small room also held a tiny closet with a row of shelves down one of the inside walls. It was fortunate Daisy had very little clothing to store in the cubbyhole.

The front room had a hide-a-bed sofa, and Mrs. McKay showed Daisy how to pull it out. The fabric on it was not new, but it was clean and comfortable, even if the odd shade of yellow did clash with the golden rug.

A small metal table with one painted navy blue wooden chair sat in the kitchen area. One counter had a sink. The other had an abbreviated refrigerator under it that wasn't even three feet tall. The "stove" was a hot plate and a toaster oven.

Cream-colored lace curtains covered the windows, and cheap pictures hung on the walls. Daisy, who had visited the finest art galleries and museums in Europe, thought the roses and kittens were adorable. Pots and pans and dishes nestled in the cupboards; towels and sheets sat on the shelves in the bathroom closet. Daisy was enchanted, and Mrs. McKay was happy to have a new tenant, even a noncommunicative one.

Mrs. McKay wanted to stay and talk, but Daisy was just as determined to get the scarf off her head and a new color in her hair. She told Mrs. McKay that she wanted to get settled in and go after that job at the café as soon as possible. The friendly landlady reluctantly gave up and left cross-examining her new tenant for another day.

Daisy liked the way her hair turned out. The new color seemed to add some body along with the rich, warm, reddish brown tint. She put on the new dress and admired herself in the full-length mirror on the bathroom door. Peter had chosen a soft flower print with a gathered skirt. The narrow belt fastened with a big gold buckle. Daisy smiled to herself. This was the first belt she'd had in three years; patients at the Estate were not allowed to have belts, since belts could be used for a suicide attempt. The dress was finished off with a broad white collar edged in lace and sleeves that came to just above the elbows, ending in a white cuff with the same edging of lace.

She was pleased with what she saw and wished she could show Peter. Daisy firmly reminded herself that she could not see Mr. Hudson. She didn't know him and she was supposed to be on her own.

She still wanted to do a few more things. The variety store was the closest of her stops, so she went there first. She bought makeup, underthings, two skirts, and three blouses. A sweater and a pair of jeans seemed necessary and a flannel nightgown.

Her next stop was her little house to fix up her face and put away her purchases. She hung up the clothes in the bathroom closet. *I ought to get rid of the Estate dress,* she thought, but she didn't know what to do with it. She hung it in the back of the closet and headed out to find the café.

Daisy walked through the café's door a little after four o'clock A HELP WANTED sign still hung in the window. Daisy asked the waitress standing by the register about the job.

"My name's Polly," the friendly woman greeted her. "I'll take you to O'Brien. He's the owner and he's the cook, too. He's an old grouch. Don't let him scare you."

O'Brien glared at her and asked a few questions, but he didn't seem much interested in the answers.

At last, he turned to Polly. "Show her the ropes and get her a couple of uniforms."

She had the job, and she could start with the dinner crowd.

The gray uniform had maroon piping. One uniform was too big, but it would pass. The other fit well, but the girl who had worn it before had shortened the skirt considerably. Daisy chose to wear the one that was too big.

Polly steered her through the first scary night with lots of advice and encouragement. Daisy tried not to let her nervousness show. At ten o'clock, O'Brien sent her home with Roy, the busboy. Daisy sat back on the cracked vinyl seat of the old wreck of a car and happily let him escort her. This big and enthusiastic high school kid gabbed on about everything. Not only did his size dwarf the petite new waitress, but his monologue bowled her over. He talked all six blocks to the McKays'. By the time they pulled in the drive, Daisy knew about his girlfriend and her age and ambitions, his age — sixteen — his new driver's license, and his madness for basketball. She liked him and enjoyed his engaging foolishness.

The days went by and Daisy did not see Peter. She did learn about him from Polly.

"I saw Peter Hudson's back from Denver," she heard Polly tell a customer.

"He didn't bring back a bride like his father, did he?" the lady laughed.

"No, he's as single as ever, and after his

daddy's big boo-boo, he may stay single forever," answered Polly.

When the woman was gone, Daisy found a chance to ask, "Who's Peter Hudson?"

"He runs the Bar 26 Ranch now that his father is retired. It's a huge spread. I forget how many thousands and thousands of acres. It's a real old ranch, goes back to a Spanish grant or something. Anyway, he's okay, pretty nice guy. They say he has other interests besides cattle, and that worries some folks. If he goes running around after all that other business stuff, he might neglect the ranch and let it fail. Not likely, though — family tradition and honor and all that kind of thing are big with the Hudsons. He's clever enough to keep the place going while juggling all the other business. He's smart."

"Why did that lady say that about bringing a bride back from Denver?"

"She was joking about the second Mrs. Ray Hudson. The first one, the mother of all the kids, died fifteen years ago, just when I was getting out of high school. Three years ago, Mr. Hudson went to Denver for a week of business and came back married to a girl younger than his son and his oldest daughter. Now, those two gallivant all over the world, and Peter runs the ranch. Folks say Mr. Ray is ashamed to be seen with her in his own town. She's spoiled and demanding and can throw some real fits."

That was all Daisy was to learn about her benefactor or his family for awhile. If Peter Hudson was keeping an eye on her, he was staying true to his word and not allowing anyone to know.

The first week of work was hard. At the Estate, she had done little but walk aimlessly about. Daisy found that she was exhausted every night when Roy took her home.

Chapter 9

Peter intended to wait until he'd heard from his uncle before he made contact with Daisy again. He hoped he'd bring her good news, that everything was not as black as she imagined, and his lawyer uncle had figured out a way to help her.

One night as he drove through town late, he noticed the lights of the diner. He had heard they had a new waitress there, and he knew it must be Daisy. At a quarter before ten, it would be closed soon. He fought the urge to see her right now, talk with her right now, and hear all that she had been through since he had left her on the road. He could go in for a cup of coffee, only that would be strange, since he had never done such a thing before. Peter told himself there was time enough later, and she'd be mad at him for trying to see her. It was foolish, an unnecessary risk. He parked down the road to wait and watch.

He had purposely kept away. He had hoped if he didn't see her, he could dispel the strong emotion that drove him to protect her. It hadn't worked. Now, he waited in his dark car, lurking in the shadows, of all things. He just wanted to see that she was all right, though. He wouldn't offer her a lift or anything so foolhardy. This was a very small town, and someone would be bound to see them. Nobody did anything without it going through the grapevine. He'd just sit and . . . and maybe there would be an opportunity.

A couple of minutes before closing, Roy came out with Daisy right behind. They walked to the kid's car and got in. Peter followed them to the McKays' and again parked down the street, this time in the shadows of a huge old weeping willow. Still, he worried that someone would spot his familiar car.

Roy left as soon as Daisy was in the little house. Peter assumed from the direction he was going that he was on his way back to the café. The big McKay house was dark. The neighborhood was quiet.

Peter decided he couldn't chance a visit to Daisy. He turned on his ignition and drove home. Inside, Sidney leaped up to greet him, delightfully surprised when his master grabbed the leash and took him out for a late walk. They walked the ten blocks back to the McKays'.

Peter allowed Sidney to snuffle under the bushes as they passed. The deserted road probably had no witnesses to his nocturnal rambling, but if anyone did see him, they would just think he was out for a stroll with his dog.

Daisy was going to be irritated to see him, but he'd deal with that as it came. Man and dog crept up the driveway of the McKays' silent home and went through the backyard.

"Well, Sidney, you're a better watchdog than Mrs. McKay's old hound," Peter told his companion, thanking God that the other dog must be sound asleep.

He knocked softly on the door of the little white house.

She opened the door almost immediately. "Peter," she exclaimed. Her voice was surprised, and the door held firmly in place was unfriendly. "I thought it was Roy. That I'd forgotten something, or he wanted to tell me one more time that everything would be okay."

"Let me in before someone sees me," Peter urged.

"No," she said. "Why are you here?"

"Because I want to talk to you, and you haven't got a phone."

"Go away."

"No," he returned. "I'm not going away until I talk to you. You'd better let me in."

She opened the door, and he stepped in, bringing a curious Sidney with him. Daisy looked down at the dog but made no comment. She walked over to the other side of the tiny room and fiddled with the curtain on the window.

Peter realized that she wasn't behaving as she ought. She was nervous. What worried him more was she kept sneaking looks at him as if she expected him to pounce on her. She seemed to think she had to keep an eye on him. Dear Lord, what's the matter? How could he help her if she'd decided he was the bogeyman?

In the light of the small living room, he saw how pale and distraught she was. She'd probably been crying earlier, though her eyes were dry now.

"What's the matter?" he asked abruptly.

"Why are you here?" She threw him a look of distrust.

"I thought we were friends. Why are you acting this way?"

"How am I acting?" she countered petulantly.

"Like I'm going to attack you."

"Men are beastly," she said emphatically. Her angry eyes met his puzzled ones.

Peter nodded as if in full agreement with Daisy's assessment of his fellowman. He willingly condemned all of his gender. "Why don't you tell me what happened?"

"Polly says to just keep the target well out of range, so I've been trying to stand farther away from the tables when I'm serving male customers. O'Brien says I'm too sensitive. You've just got to expect that sort of thing and not make a federal case out of it."

Daisy paced up and down in front of the kitchen area now. She wrapped her arms tightly across her chest as if she were cold.

Peter silently wondered if he were picking up the clues properly and deciphering correctly the message she was sending.

"The pinches and pats I've learned to avoid now, but the first few days were terrible." She stopped by the couch and picked up a fringed throw pillow. She hugged it, avoiding Peter's eyes. "Tonight there were two guys left in the diner. I was cleaning up tables, and they called me over for their check. I had a pitcher of ice water in my hand. I was standing there talking to one of them, when the other one dropped his napkin. He leaned over to pick it up, only he put his hand on the inside of my

84

ankle and came up my leg and under my skirt."

"What did you do?" Peter kept his voice remarkably calm in light of the rage bolting through him. Sidney responded to the underlying emotion in Peter's voice and came to his feet.

"I screamed and dumped the ice water over his head. Then I ran for the kitchen. Only I threw the pitcher up in the air, and when it came down, it landed on the tray of glasses I'd collected, and they went everywhere. I'd put the tray down on their table to tear out their check. There were broken glass and ice cubes and water all over the place."

"What did O'Brien do?"

"He went out and apologized to them! He mopped them up himself. The men were all wet and he was wiping them up and agreeing with them that I was a stupid female. He took them to the register and checked them out himself. Then he came back to the kitchen and told me I was a fool, and if I ever created such a scene when the diner was crowded, or for that matter, ever again, I'd be canned. Polly yelled at him, and Roy said it wasn't fair, so they both got yelled at, too."

"What did you do?"

"I cried. O'Brien said it was obvious I wasn't going to be any more help tonight. He yelled at Roy to take me home."

Sidney shuffled over to sit at the distressed girl's feet. She bent over and placed a hand on his silken head. His truly sympathetic gaze met hers. No one can offer as much sympathy with a look as a well-bred basset.

"I like your hair," Peter said.

"What?" Daisy looked up.

"Your hair. The color is nice. I like the way you fixed it, too."

Unconsciously, she reached up a hand to touch the soft braid in the back.

"It's called a French braid. Polly helped me do it, and she cut the bangs. I've never had hair this long, and I've never had bangs. I'm thinking about getting a permanent," she added.

"No, don't do that," he said. "When you leave here, you ought to have some money in your pocket, so you can lay over a day someplace to work on changing your identity. That's when you should do things like permanents." She listened intently. Seeing her absorbed in this possibility, he went on. "Also, you should chuck the clothes you wore the most, your favorite blouse, things like that."

"That's a good idea."

"Did you get some new clothes?"

Her face brightened with enthusiasm, and Peter once again thanked God for all the tactical training he had had, not in the Marines, but in dealing with his sisters.

"Yes, but I've hardly had a chance to wear them. I wear the uniform mostly. One is way too short."

"Mrs. McKay sews. See if she will help you take the hem out or something. Let me see what you bought."

"How do you know Mrs. McKay sews?" she asked as she went into the bathroom to the closet.

Peter sat down on the couch. Sidney settled at his feet.

"She made prom dresses for my sisters."

Daisy came out with a skirt and two blouses. The broomstick skirt had vibrant colors, a floral print. The blouses were soft and feminine. One was white with big, billowy sleeves and a broad collar. The other was pink with a tight little collar and straight sleeves that buttoned at the cuffs. Both the collar and the cuffs were trimmed neatly with a thin band of lace.

"I can wear both of these with the skirt."

Peter nodded agreeably. "They're very pretty. Were you able to get anything else?"

That sent her back to fetch another outfit. It was a denim skirt with a peach, country-cut blouse. She'd bought a matching peach scarf to tie around her waist.

Peter approved again and asked her if she had anything to drink. She offered tea. Peter said he'd take a cup if she didn't mind. Daisy saw the smile quirk the corner of his mouth and she knew he'd manipulated her, but she found she didn't care.

While she was fixing the tea, Peter stewed. Obviously, she was not capable of fending for herself. She was too trusting. Even after her scare at the diner, she had let him in. Of course, she should trust him, but it showed a too gullible nature that she just let him talk his way in the door. The more he thought about it, the more he could see that an unscrupulous fellow would be in seventh heaven with her. He couldn't let her fall into the hands of one of the local Don Juans.

When she sat beside him on the couch, he played for time by introducing his dog.

"My sisters gave him to me as a puppy when I returned from my hitch with the Marines. They felt the responsibility of owning a dog would keep me closer to home. That's what they said, anyway. I think they fell in love with him first and then thought of an excuse to keep him."

Daisy smiled down at the likable dog and reached to rub his ears. Sidney rewarded her by leaning against her leg.

Peter decided the time was right to lay out the plan he had just conceived.

"Daisy, you are going to become my girl."

She turned those wide dark eyes to his face. She wore a trace of makeup, and her hair glimmered in the light of the lamp behind the couch. He caught his breath at the sight and took a sip of the hot tea to distract himself.

"What do you mean?"

"Tomorrow I am going to come to the diner and 'meet' you for the first time. We'll take it from there. But this is the point of this maneuver — if I'm chasing you, that will put off some of the local yokels. At least, as big brother to the three gorgeous Hudson girls, I served the purpose of cooling some of their unwanted suitors. It could work in this situation."

"You don't mind?" she asked.

Peter nearly groaned out loud. She needed to be locked up for her safety.

To the best of his ability, he answered in a serious tone. "No, not a bit."

When he and Sidney left her, he promised to see her in the afternoon at the café. She told him where to sit so that it would be one of the tables she covered.

At two-thirty, Peter Hudson walked into Dooley's only eatery. He said he was waiting for someone, but he'd take a cup of coffee. He seemed to ignore Daisy, and she went about her business.

Polly grabbed her arm behind the counter and whispered, "That's Peter Hudson."

Daisy lifted her eyebrows in mock surprise. "I thought rich ranchers were older and a little bald."

Polly giggled. "Well, his father is, and he has a slightly rounder belly, too. But so far, Rich Cattleman Jr. is holding up all right."

"How old do you think he is?" asked Daisy.

"I know he's twenty-nine because he graduated two years after I did from high school."

Mr. Hudson, rich cattle rancher, called her back to the table and asked her for a piece of pie. He scarcely looked up from the papers he was studying. Daisy filled up his coffee cup without being asked.

A little after three, he waved her over, asking for his check.

"Look," he said, "I was supposed to meet a man here, and he didn't show. Maybe he had car trouble. Anyway, his name is Mick Bigelow. I don't know what he looks like, but if someone comes in looking for me, would you ask his name and send this Bigelow fellow down to my office?"

"Sure," answered Daisy. "Where's your office?"

Peter looked up at her, somewhat surprised. "It's down the street on the left. The sign says Hudson Bar 26. It's next to the barber shop."

"Oh, I've seen it," Daisy acknowledged.

"You aren't from around here, are you?"

She shook her head.

"What's your name?"

"Daisy Madden."

"Welcome to Dooley, Daisy," Peter said smoothly, his smile charming and his eyes friendly. "I'm Peter Hudson."

"Thank you, Sir." She walked away.

Peter strolled to the end of the diner and spoke for a few minutes to a couple of men who were enjoying a coffee break. When he went to the register, Polly took his check and rang him up. They exchanged a few

91

pleasant words. He started to leave as Daisy came out of the back, her hands full with a huge tray that carried five dinner plates. She was on the way to the family seated in the corner booth.

He caught her eye and spoke, "It was nice to meet you, Dixie."

He left abruptly as if he had business to attend to. Polly laughed, "Well, at least he noticed you, Dixie. I'd be willing to change my name for one of his smiles."

"I'm not planning to change my name anytime soon," Daisy replied, aware of the irony of the statement. "Daisy has suited me well for as long as I've had it." She hurried to the customers whose baby was beginning to squall.

Later that day, when they were busy with the dinner crowd, O'Brien frowned his fiercest as his three waitresses gathered around the florist box that had been delivered for Daisy.

"The box says Cutter's. That's in Browmere. It's the nearest flower shop with any class," said Gayle.

"Browmere is about twice as big as Dooley," added Polly. "Look at this box. It's straight out of the movies. There should be a dozen long-stemmed red roses in it."

"Hurry up and open it," urged Gayle.

"Yes," bellowed O'Brien. "Hurry up!"

Daisy slipped the blue ribbon and bow to the end of the box and handed it to Polly. She lifted the lid and the two girls exclaimed together, "Daisies!"

"Wow!" said Gayle. "There must be three dozen. Where are you ever going to get a vase that big?"

"Look how gigantic they are. They must be a special kind." Polly started digging around in the folds of the green paper that wrapped the stems. "Here's the card. Read it, Daisy."

Daisy opened the tiny envelope and pulled out the card. She read aloud, "Was halfway down the street when I realized my mistake, Daisy. This is so I won't slip again. Please accept my apology. Peter."

"Wow!" said Gayle.

"I'm going to 'wow' all of you if you don't get on these orders," came O'Brien's rough, angry tones from the kitchen. The girls jumped.

Fifteen minutes later, Daisy saw that someone had put her flowers in one of the diner's huge glass pitchers. They looked rather nice, if a bit crowded, on the counter next to the register.

Polly and Gayle were excited and Daisy

was very quiet. Roy was the one who had found time to put the flowers in water, and he persuaded O'Brien to let her take the pitcher home when they left that night.

When he took her home, he said, "I'm going to go to college and get a real job that pays big money. Then, I'm going to send a giant bunch of flowers to whatever girl is the girl of my dreams at the moment. You should have seen your face when you opened that box."

Chapter 10

The telephone rang. Peter put down the papers he was reading and reached across his desk to pick up the receiver.

"Hello," he said.

"Hello, yourself," came the answer.

"Uncle Henry." Peter sat up, shaken from his relaxed attitude. "What did you learn?"

"I'm fine, thank you. And your aunt and cousins are doing well. Little Bobby has had the measles, but he's recovered nicely." Uncle Henry's voice was full of his particular brand of droll humor.

"Uncle Henry," Peter replied sternly, "I have been waiting for almost two weeks. Cut the funny business and tell me what you've found out."

Uncle Henry became serious. "Peter, if your gal is the one we think she is, she has got problems. First, if the background put out about her is true, she's a psychological mess and you wouldn't want to touch her with a ten-foot pole. Then, there's the other side, which is the one I lean toward. She's been given a raw deal. If my suspicions are correct, she is in a very dangerous situation."

"I'll bet it's the second scenario, Uncle Henry." Concern permeated Peter's voice. "Clue me in."

"We think she is Julie Jones. She spent the last three years in a place called the French Estate Private Hospital. She was initially admitted for trying to commit suicide overdosing on sleeping pills. The family had not been aware of a drug problem because she was schooled abroad. She has always been in boarding schools or under escort as she roamed through Europe.

"Our detective romanced an attendant from the hospital and discovered the girl had turned up missing. She was reported to the police, and private detectives were put on the trail. The attendant says the girl was calm and no trouble recently, but the first year she was a wild, hysterical patient. Of course, Dr. French's treatments have helped a lot, but it is still believed that she is highly suicidal.

"Peter, it is my belief that if they find her, she will conveniently die by her own hand."

"Why?" Peter asked in horror.

"She was put in that hospital by her

uncle and declared incompetent. He has control of the business left to her. A very lucrative business, by the way. I've had the uncle checked out. His name is Jacob Jones. He is not a nice man either in business or at home."

"Mafia?" Peter questioned.

"He has no compunctions with whom he does business, but he is really a small fish in their eyes and on the outside of their close-knit circle."

"Well, I guess that's something to be thankful for. Where does he live?"

"New York. But the home ground is Indiana."

"I didn't think anybody with really big money came out of Indiana."

Uncle Henry laughed. "Apparently, he doesn't, either. And he wants to be as rich and powerful as they come, so he moved on to more promising ground. He's beginning to have a very strong hand in government. If his niece is found and her inheritance restored, he will lose three-quarters of his wealth."

"What do you suggest?"

"Do you think the girl is crazy?"

"Naïve and gullible, but not crazy," Peter returned.

"If she comes out to claim her inheritance, she's got to have help. They could whip her out of sight and into another hospital. Or she could have another suicide attempt that doesn't fail. The court has awarded her uncle protective custody. We wouldn't have a legal foot to stand on if he opted to take her away. As it is now, he'd be doing it for her own good in the eyes of the law."

"What are we going to do?"

"Well, we're going to have to prove her case before they find her. I'm already working on that. I think I can get enough evidence to unmask that phony hospital. I wonder how many other rich patients are incarcerated there. I'll work on that, and you work on keeping her out of sight and safe."

"Right. How long is this going to take?"

"I've no idea, Peter."

Peter had been to the diner twice, but he chose times when he knew Daisy would not be there. This caused the talk he wanted. He'd never been a regular customer of the diner and it was suspicious that he should start popping in. The gossips of the town were speculating, and that suited him fine.

The third trip, he caught her at work,

and as he left, he asked her when her day off was.

"Tomorrow," she answered.

"I'm going to Corpus tomorrow. How about going with me, and I'll take you out to dinner?"

"I'd like that," she said demurely. A quizzical little smile played at the corner of her mouth, and her eyes twinkled with secret laughter. He looked at her and wondered what kind of monster would want to hurt her.

"Fine. I'll pick you up at nine-thirty tomorrow morning. Is that too early? I have to do some business in town."

"That's fine, but don't you want to know where I live?"

He laughed. "You haven't ever lived in a town this small before. I found out where you lived the day after I met you."

He left, and Polly and Gayle descended upon her.

"Wow!" said Gayle. "You play your cards right, Honey," she advised. "He's worth something. Not just money, either. He's a nice guy."

"Why didn't he come to my house to ask me out?" Daisy asked.

Polly shrugged. "Who knows for sure? Maybe because of nosy Mrs. McKay, although they know each other fairly well. Most of us know Mrs. McKay. She taught Sunday school for years. Anyone who grew up in Bayside Church had a couple of years of her, stories and all."

Gayle hadn't attended the Bayside Church so she had a different opinion. "Maybe he thought you'd be spooked if he just showed up at your door. I mean, think how awkward it would be. You couldn't just ask in someone who is practically a stranger."

Polly agreed. "He's never been the rich playboy type. But you wouldn't know that. He could have been thinking of your reputation, too."

"You're going to have the reputation for being out of work if you don't stop jawing and get busy!" A familiar bellow interrupted the girls' conversation.

Daisy continued to think about what the other two had said. What would they think of her adventure on the road when Peter picked her up, fed her, gave her a place to sleep, and gave her money and clothes? Thinking along the lines of not even letting a "stranger" into her little house, Daisy thought perhaps she had been even more blessed by God than she realized. Her story might have been a lot different if a villain had come to her aid instead of a hero.

Chapter 11

Dark clouds and a chilly wind had turned the day dreary when Peter knocked on Daisy's door the next morning. She wore the dress he had picked out for her and the sweater from the Estate.

"Is that all you've got to keep warm?" he asked her gruffly.

"Coats are expensive," she answered.

"Well, we'll look for one in Corpus."

"You can't buy me a coat," Daisy objected.

"I didn't intend to. Do you have your money with you?"

She shook her head.

"Daisy, no woman from Dooley goes to Corpus without her pocketbook as full as she can get it. Go back in and get your money."

She returned shortly, clutching her purse.

"Was it under the mattress?" he asked.

"No, folded in the sheets in the closet. I kept it in the hide-a-bed last week." She looked up at him with that complete lack of duplicity that wrenched his heart. In order to relieve the pain, he bent over, brushing his lips quickly and gently across hers. She gave a small gasp. Her eyes widened and her mouth fell open just a tiny bit, enough to accentuate her attraction.

"Oh," he groaned and grabbed her by the arm, propelling her down the backyard sidewalk to the driveway where he was parked. "Let's get moving. I'm drowning."

"What?" she asked, not sure she heard him right.

"Nothing," he responded. "I'll have my Uncle Henry explain it to you someday."

On the way to Corpus Christi, Peter outlined his plans for the day. They'd eat lunch first, since it took about two hours to get there and that would put them in Corpus at lunchtime. Then he had a business meeting at one. He'd called his sister Lisa, and she was going to meet them at the museum. Daisy and Lisa could go shopping together while he worked.

"Is that a good idea?" Daisy wondered aloud.

"I thought shopping was always a good idea." Peter was puzzled.

"I mean meeting your sister. I'm not supposed to make a lot of friends who could accidentally betray me."

"Don't give her any information."

"I've gotten good at that." Daisy grinned with mischief in her eye.

"You have?"

"Yes." Daisy giggled, pleasing Peter's heart. "Mrs. McKay gives me lots of practice. She comes over bound and determined to find out all about me. I ask her one question about one of her kids, though, and I'm safe for an hour and a half. I'll bet I could write that woman's family history."

Peter laughed, too. His knowledge of the dear lady backed up Daisy's claim.

"It works a charm on everyone," Daisy continued. "Polly is always curious, but her boyfriends are more interesting than where I came from and what I used to do."

"The reason I want you to hang around my sister," explained Peter, "is because it ruins the image of a lady with a mysterious past. Would I take you to go shopping with my sister if I had even a suspicion of something shady in your past?"

"Peter." The tone of her voice made him turn to look at her. "How do you know I don't?"

He pulled the car to the side of the road and turned off the engine. He prayed that she was ready to tell him the truth. He sat with his hands on the wheel, giving the moment to God before he turned back to look into those questioning eyes. He had no idea what to tell her. If he told her he knew the truth, he would also have to tell her how much danger she was in. If she took off like a scared rabbit, how was he going to even begin to protect her? He was frightened to think how unguarded she was, even with him watching from a distance.

He put his arm around her shoulders, drawing her closer to him. His hand cupped under her chin, he tilted her head just a little more in order to receive his kiss. It was a soft kiss, but her lips warmed beneath his and responded. He tightened his hold on her and felt the need to always be her guardian. Her arms came around his neck, and he knew she was enjoying the same warmth that he was.

He pulled back and looked at her. Her cheeks were flushed rosy and her eyes had a dreamy, unfocused look.

"Understand?" he asked.

She nodded. Abruptly her expression changed. She sat up, drawing away from him.

"No, I don't understand," she said.

"I trust you because I've opened up my life to you. Without trusting you, I wouldn't have allowed you into the position where you could hurt me. I don't expect you to be perfect or to have a past without a blemish. I do expect you to hold this trust with the care I know you are capable of. I know you would never deliberately hurt me any more than I would hurt you."

"It scares me," she said.

"Why?"

"It's not part of my plan."

"Daisy, check that plan out with God. I know you believe in Him, but do you trust Him? Are you giving Him all your troubles, the big ones and the day-to-day ones?"

"Trust again." She sighed.

"Love and trust are bound together."

"I figure God's taking care of anyone looking for me. I think He expects me to take care of myself."

"He expects you to depend on Him in every area. He's a God who takes care of details. Do you know in the Bible it says when the fisherman brought in that unbelievable catch, there were 153 large fish? Mrs. McKay taught me that story — and she said God knew about little boys because every year the boys wanted to know how many fish there were, and God included the information.

"He cares about lost coins, wine at a wedding. Yes, He raised Lazarus from the dead, but He also stopped to be friendly to children. Trust Him with all the little details."

Daisy listened to Peter. She had rarely had anyone with whom to discuss her ideas about Christianity. She wanted time to think about what he had said.

Peter heaved a sigh. He didn't know how well he had expressed his beliefs. Had he reached beyond that fence she had guarding her heart?

"Daisy, let me help with your plans."

"For a little while," she said guardedly.

Peter fought the urge to lay into her with arguments and logic and all the things that lost battles for him when he handled his sisters.

"Okay," he said. He turned on the engine. They continued their journey. He prayed they were on the right path. He prayed they could go through life on one path, so that when one fell, the other would be there to help.

They ate at a seafood restaurant. Peter explained that to have all new clothes whenever she turned up someplace would be conspicuous. Shopping at Goodwill or

Salvation Army would be cheaper and the clothes from these places would be less noticeable.

Peter left her in his sister's care, instructing both girls to go to Goodwill first. Lisa was a wiry girl with dark, flashing eyes and bouncing brown hair.

"Humph!" said Lisa as her older brother drove away. "He's always like that, Daisy. He orders you around like you couldn't make one decision for yourself."

"No, I need to shop at Goodwill, Lisa," Daisy explained. "I don't have much money and I need a winter coat. He was just telling you where I wanted to go."

"Well, don't let him bully you. He has a big-brother complex. Anything small and feminine ought to be bossed around. He lost more girlfriends that way in college. We were at school together for a few years, but would he listen to advice from a little sister?"

"I'm glad he didn't. He might have been married by now."

"Oh, ho!" exclaimed Lisa with a glimmer of triumph in her eye. She was always happy to ferret out information on her older brother. As much as she liked to tease him, she loved him and was concerned over his perpetual bachelorhood.

"Does he have it as bad for you as you do for him?"

"I don't know," answered Daisy truthfully.

"No girl ever does," observed Lisa sagely. "But, I'll tell you that my brother is a good egg even though he comes on strong as the mighty protector of the weak and lowly. He'd make a great husband and father."

"I don't know if it will ever get that far." Daisy had a worried look in her eye. "It would take a miracle to work out all the details. And I don't think I could be weak and lowly for the rest of my life."

"That's a good show of spirit." Lisa laughed and then gave her attention to the traffic for a few minutes as she maneuvered through a narrow street. When she spoke again, she was serious.

"I believe in a God that is still doing miracles, do you?"

"Yes," said Daisy. "Definitely."

"Then He'll take care of those details. Where do you want to shop?"

"Goodwill," answered Daisy.

"All right," Lisa conceded. "Goodwill first, but then we'll go someplace I choose."

They met Peter at the appointed hour

and transferred Daisy's purchases to his car trunk.

"Did you buy out the stores?" questioned Peter.

"No, your friend here needs lessons in shopping with abandon," said Lisa.

"And I know the expert who would volunteer to instruct her in the finer arts of blowing a wad," returned Peter.

Lisa laughed. "Why don't you two come home and eat dinner with John and me? It'll make you late getting home, but we'd love to have you."

Peter looked at Daisy and raised his eyebrows, questioning. She nodded.

"Okay, we'll follow you."

It was the first time Daisy had eaten in someone's home since she had been sent away to school. At first, she felt shy, but Lisa lured her into the kitchen and set her to work making the salad. When Lisa next paid attention to what her guest was doing, her eyes popped.

"That's some salad," she exclaimed, looking at the big bowl artistically arranged with flowered radishes, curled carrots, celery frayed at the end to look like wands, bell peppers cut in rings with cherry tomatoes as centers, and cauliflower buds accentuating their colors.

"I went to cooking school once. I really did well in soups, but I almost flunked pastries. I made an apple pie that the senior chef couldn't put his fork through."

"How are you on gravy?"

"Clear or creamed?"

"Clear," said Lisa.

"Let me at it. I finally conquered lumps in the other, but it's been too long. I'd probably produce something that looked akin to dumplings."

The two couples enjoyed the dinner; and when they left, Peter stopped so they could walk on the beach before they went home. Beautiful moonlight did nothing to offset the bone-chilling cold, but Daisy wore her Goodwill coat. The quilted fabric reached down past her knees, and the nylon fabric rustled as she walked. She shivered.

Peter noticed and gathered her into his arms.

"It's crazy to be walking out here tonight, but I just don't want to take you back yet." He kissed her, and when she pulled away from him, he was surprised.

"I don't want to fall in love with you, Peter," she pleaded, as if he could do something about it.

"Isn't it too late?" he asked. She didn't

answer. He gave her a little shake. "Answer me. Isn't it too late?"

"Yes," she admitted and threw her arms around his neck.

Chapter 12

The diner would be closed for Thanksgiving. Peter's sisters, by tradition, always tried to be home for the holiday, and Peter had invited Daisy to the feast.

He was happy with the prospect, but he soon detected a note of reserve in Daisy's attitude.

"What's the matter?" he asked. They sat on her couch, and Sidney had persuaded her with his typical woebegone expression to allow him up on the couch as well. He lounged in luxury with his head in her lap.

Peter didn't want to leave Daisy even though the hour was growing late. This was not unusual. The talk of the town was how hard the cattleman had fallen. They had been dating for three weeks, and where he went, she went. He took her to church; he took her grocery shopping; when he could, he ate breakfast, lunch, and dinner at the café. She traveled with him on her days off, riding in the pickup over the range or tagging along as he did business in the neighboring towns. Now

Peter Hudson, cattleman, had two faithful companions: the furry beast they were used to seeing and the much more beautiful waitress from O'Brien's diner.

"What do you mean?" she asked.

"Every time I mention Thanksgiving, you get tense," he explained.

"You have so much family." She tried to explain. "The only ones I know are John and Lisa. It's a bit overwhelming to meet so many people at once, and I really don't know much about Thanksgiving."

"You don't know much about Thanksgiving?" Peter sounded incredulous.

"No, I never . . ." She broke off. This was leading to dangerous territory. In Europe, Thanksgiving wasn't celebrated. "We didn't do holidays much in our house." That was certainly true. Daisy hedged further. "There didn't seem much point when there wasn't any love."

Peter remained quiet. Maybe she was ready to tell him the truth.

"There wasn't ever anybody to share that sort of thing. All this is foreign to me as if it were the custom of a different country." Again the many lonely holidays spent abroad grew vivid in her memory. "Does it make sense to tell you it makes me homesick? It makes me homesick for things that happened before I was eight years old, and I really don't have many clear memories of that time."

Peter hugged her to him. "Tell me what it was like. What did you do for holidays?"

She jumped out of his arms. Sidney slid to the floor and gave her a disgusted look; she usually was very polite about removing him from her lap before she got up. Daisy paced the floor.

Peter watched in growing frustration. He wanted to catch her and make her give up all the pretense that stood between them.

"I can't, Peter," she cried.

Her desperation crumbled his resolve. He stood up and intercepted her. She grasped his arms tightly in her hands and looked earnestly into his eyes.

"I can't lie to you anymore, Peter. I just can't tell you even one more lie. So much of what you know about me is half-truths. I can't tell you anything at all."

"Why can't you tell me the truth?" he asked quietly.

"Because I love you."

"That doesn't make sense, Daisy." He tried to keep the irritation out of his voice. "I love you, and taking care of you is a God-given responsibility that comes along with that love."

"You might get in trouble, too."

"I'm a big boy," he said, trying to lighten her mood. "Let me tackle the troubles."

She looked down at the floor and shook her head sadly. He came very close to shaking her. His failure to break through her reluctance to include him in all her life chafed against the patience he knew he must maintain.

He gathered her in his arms and held her fiercely. *God, I need Your control. Tell me what to say, what to do.*

"Peter." Daisy interrupted his silent prayer. "Would you go home now? I can't think when you're here, and I'm all mixed up."

He was silent, not answering. Finally, she looked up to find him watching her.

"Please," she said.

He nodded, his face stern and his jaw set.

"Please don't look like that. I don't know what you're thinking."

"I'm thinking I should spank you."

"I don't think it would help." Her face wore a wistful smile.

"Neither do I, or you'd be across my knee this minute." He kissed her gruffly and grabbed his coat. "Don't do anything foolish, Daisy. Remember your promise.

You won't ever leave without saying good-bye."

"I remember."

He left, feeling unsettled.

Thanksgiving Day, he picked Daisy up at ten. She had asked him what to wear, and he had suggested the flowered skirt and a blouse would fit in with what his sisters would be wearing. When they arrived out at the country ranch house, she immediately noted the sisters wore casual clothing, nice but casual.

Lisa took her around to introduce her, and the feeling of being out of place soon passed. A Hudson family trait was hospitality. She felt accepted by the members of Peter's family.

Scram was nearly as tall as Peter. Lisa said she stole all the height in the family, just as she had stolen everybody's makeup or hair curlers or anything else she had needed.

Tiger and Tabitha won her heart.

"If we are really, really good," Tabitha confided, "we get to stay up late and listen to the grown-ups talk."

Tiger nodded solemnly and added, "If we blow it, we get a spanking."

"You got that right," affirmed his father, Joe, good-naturedly.

Lovely and sophisticated Midge spoke with more reserve than her sisters. She had a warm smile and welcomed Daisy generously, but she didn't have that lively sense of humor that bubbled out of the other two sisters. Daisy labeled her serene in her mind. Midge's husband, Mike, was quiet, too.

The surprise was the presence of Uncle Henry and Aunt Harriet, who was often called Aunt Harry. They had their eight-year-old grandson, Bobby, with them. They had decided to join the family gathering because Uncle Henry had some business to discuss with Peter, and it had been too long since he'd seen his future law partner, Midge.

Lisa hauled Daisy into the kitchen of the house where Peter had grown up. Their father's home stood empty most of the time, but the girls had thrown it open for the holiday and brought in a supply of groceries.

"Dad and Suzanne are rarely here anymore," Lisa explained. "And I don't think Suzanne is too keen on cooking when she is here. They were in Florida a week ago. Dad called to say hello. I told him about you."

"About me? What could you tell him

about me?" inquired Daisy as she peeled potatoes.

"That Peter had finally found someone who seemed willing enough to be perpetually bossed."

"Peter really doesn't do that," Daisy defended.

"Humph!" replied Lisa. "I think love has put wax in your ears."

"He just knows so much more than I do." Daisy tried another tactic.

"Oh, brother," exclaimed Lisa. "No wonder you've got him wrapped around your little finger."

Lisa caught the look of confusion on Daisy's face and gave her a sisterly hug. "Don't worry, Kid," she said. "I think it's the best thing that could have happened to him."

Scram and Midge soon joined them to help in the food preparation. Frivolous talk and banter bounced around the busy room. The sisters teased and laughed without hurt feelings. Daisy enjoyed listening to their lighthearted bantering. The atmosphere in the kitchen was entirely new to her, and she loved it. She busied herself with the tasks they gave her and listened, rarely contributing to the conversation.

"Daisy," Scram spoke to her, "Lisa says you went to cooking school. Where was that?"

Daisy had heard, but she feigned absorption in her task and didn't answer.

"Hey, Daisy," Lisa hollered. Daisy turned reluctantly. "Scram has asked you twice where you went to cooking school."

"Oh . . . oh," she stammered and smiled shyly, "I was just thinking about Peter." She made sure her voice was adequately dreamy without going over the edge to ridiculous. A starry look hovered on her face. "Isn't it funny what some men will eat? Peter picks me up after work and takes me home. Almost every night he stays and has scrambled eggs. I've cooked them in so many different ways, I could write an egg cookbook. His cholesterol will be sky-high. You'd think he'd get tired of scrambled eggs."

The sisters exchanged knowing looks. Daisy pretended not to notice. She'd given them two topics of conversation: men and their eating habits, or health and cholesterol. They chose what men will eat and completely forgot about where Daisy went to school. They were still talking about it when they set dinner on the table.

Daisy sat between Uncle Henry and

Peter during dinner. When they held hands with the person next to them and bowed heads to pray, she nearly cried, so moved was she by the love that flowed among them. She had heard that where three or more were gathered, Jesus was in their midst, but she had never before experienced that extraordinary warmth of fellowship. She was surprised that Uncle Henry thanked God for her presence and asked for protection and guidance for her. Again she fought the tears; only by thinking how embarrassed she would be to burst into tears among these kind people did she control the flood.

Dinner began in earnest, and Daisy covered her emotional response under the guise of passing and scooping the delicious dishes. She longed to be swallowed up by this family, forever cosseted within their circle of fellowship.

Uncle Henry quietly asked her polite questions that she turned away by encouraging him to talk about himself. This time she hungered for more information about the family because each little tidbit made her feel more connected. She still used her technique to deflect his getting to know anything about her background, but she was aware that she was establishing an affinity that was priceless to her lonely soul.

After dinner, Daisy joined the ladies in the kitchen for cleanup. Uncle Henry and Peter hid themselves away in the study to discuss business. She didn't know she was the business.

Chapter 13

"I don't think she's as dumb as you think," Uncle Henry told Peter.

"Wait, the way I remember the conversation, I particularly told you she is not dumb," he objected.

"Naïve, you said naïve. And I'm examining that adjective as well. I tried to get her to talk about herself, and I found myself telling her about our last vacation, and Bobby's loose tooth, and the Sunday school picnic last July."

Peter laughed. "She's beautiful, isn't she?"

"I assume that is a rhetorical question. She is very pretty, Peter, but she is in a lot of trouble. Is she still not telling you all?"

Peter shook his head.

"That surprises me."

Peter sighed. "I had hoped by now she would trust me."

"Are you sure it is a matter of trust, or does she love you so much she wants to protect you?" Uncle Henry asked.

"Protect me?" Peter sounded astonished by the idea.

"Yes, Peter," chided the older man. "Others in God's kingdom can be inspired by the noble desire to protect the ones they love."

"Have you found out anything useful?" Peter decided to turn down a different path of conversation.

"What we have discovered is indeed interesting."

"So tell me," demanded Peter.

"There are fifteen patients presently at the French Estate. According to our investigations, which are not complete, seven of those poor individuals have a similar history. It is most convenient for someone to have them out of the way. The someone, in each case, just happens to be paying the hefty bill."

"Can you prove it?" was Peter's urgent question.

"Some of it is circumstantial. But there is enough that is solid and too many coincidences to be ignored. By the time we take it to the district attorney, they won't have a chance."

"What about Daisy?"

"You mean Julie. She'll ride along with the others. Jacob Jones will not dare touch her. The scandal alone will protect her from future attempts."

"You don't think we can get him behind bars?"

"That's what I'm aiming for, but I'm realistic enough to know when there is that much power and money involved, things don't always turn out equitably."

"Final justice comes from God, and no one escapes that," stated Peter. He shook his head, thinking about those people dependent on plain old human justice. "Uncle Henry, how in the world do these patients get there? I mean, if I wanted to dispose of one of my darling little sisters, how would I know there was an accommodating private hospital in the panhandle of Texas that would be willing to lock away my problem for that hefty fee you mentioned?"

Uncle Henry's odd sense of humor took over. He raised his bushy eyebrows in a comical questioning attitude. "Do you suppose this man French has an advertisement in the *Wall Street Journal* or the *New York Times*?" Henry turned serious and shrugged off his facetious answer. "I can't tell you. Word of mouth, maybe."

Peter ignored his uncle's humor. "How long before it's over?"

"At least another month, Peter. We don't want to be shorthanded on evidence when we present the case. Remember, these are unscrupulous opponents. If we let them slip through our fingers, the innocent people under their authority will be further victimized.

"And we plan to present the case at several levels simultaneously. That way, if one jurisdiction has been bought out, we have another chance.

"Publicity will help as well. The scandal sheets love this kind of thing. We can use their morbid curiosity to keep things hot for the offenders. In the meantime, we don't want to lose Julie or allow any of the guilty parties to get wise and skip out."

"Uncle Henry, I think I should marry her."

"Why is that, Peter?" the lawyer responded seriously.

Peter grinned. "Well, aside from the obvious reason, I think I'd be in a better position to protect her legally. Wouldn't it be difficult to get protective custody away from a husband?"

"They could always claim you took advantage of her confused state, but, yes, we could have our own doctors examine her and prove her of sound mind."

125

Peter took in his uncle's cautious demeanor. "But . . ."

"Peter, realistically, you have not known the girl but five weeks." He held up his hand against Peter's retort. "And is it fair to her? You are her knight in shining armor. She led a very sheltered existence in Europe. She's been three years in an insane asylum. She is naïve and gullible. Your words. You've been kind to her. Does she really love you, or is she scared and grateful?"

Peter soberly gazed out of the window.

"I'll wait," he finally said.

When they rejoined the family, they found Tiger curled up asleep on the couch. Scram, Aunt Harry, Midge, and Joe were at work on a jigsaw puzzle with Daisy looking on.

"Peter, would you believe it?" Aunt Harry exclaimed. "Daisy has never done a jigsaw puzzle."

"We've been instructing her," said Scram. She turned to their pupil and intoned with the air of a great pedantic scholar, "Wise people pick out the flat edge pieces first."

"Incorrect," declared Midge in mock outrage, obviously rehashing an old argument. "Those with superior organizational skills separate by color first."

Ignoring their dramatics, Daisy reached down and stuck in a piece.

Scram abandoned the fight to recall, "Do you remember the race we had one Christmas holiday?" She turned to Daisy to explain. "We had two identical puzzles set up on two card tables, Daisy. Peter and Midge made up one team, and Lisa and I were on the other. We started at nine o'clock one morning and vowed we wouldn't leave the tables until a team won."

"Who won?" Daisy asked the obvious question.

"Nobody. Somebody let Scooter in. He was a barn cat and definitely not allowed in the house. Jake, our faithful dog, took after him, and Peter took after Jake because Mom was yelling. Dad came in to see what the trouble was, only we had set one of the tables right in front of the door, and he ran smack into it. Scooter, Jake, and Peter managed to flatten the other. The tables tipped toward each other as they fell, so the pieces were irretrievably mixed."

Tabitha's childish screeches from outside interrupted Scram's story. The little girl came barreling through the front door, her cheeks red from the cold and her face lit up with delight.

"Grandpa's coming down the road. I saw his car at the bend." She turned and raced out again, determined to be the first to greet him.

A subtle change in the room caused Daisy to look from one member of the family to the next. The spirit of joy fizzled out and was replaced by apprehension. Uneasy looks of sufferance passed between several people and others sighed, obviously resigned to the inevitable.

"I'll put some coffee on," said Aunt Harry and left for the kitchen.

"Come on, Daisy. We'll go out and meet them." Peter took her arm and guided her toward the door. He stopped at the wooden pegs on the entryway wall and pulled down her coat from among the others. He slipped it on for her and reached for his own.

"It's my father's wife, Suzanne," Peter explained *sotto voce*. "She's caused quite a few scenes at our family gatherings. No one knows quite what to expect when she arrives."

Daisy nodded. She tucked her arm in his and they went out to greet the unexpected arrivals together.

Daisy froze. The woman was, of course, older. But the remarkably beautiful face, the refined features showing the signs of a storm brewing, all were the exact likeness of the spoiled Suzanne Winthrop, who had attended Madame Melanz's conservatory many years ago. Her cool gray eyes under the streaks of perfectly arched black brows still reflected that thoughtless attitude that had caused many vulnerable girls to steer clear of her. Suzanne Winthrop might be ten years older and Mrs. Ray Hudson, but she was still a pouting brat.

For a fleeting moment, Julie Jones was afraid she would be recognized. She set the fear aside. She had been a lowly eleven-year-old, far beneath the imperious sixteen-year-old beauty's notice. Julie Jones had only been at that conservatory three months. Suzanne Hudson would never be a threat.

Chapter 14

Ray Hudson's attention was claimed by the enthusiastic welcome of his granddaughter, Tabitha. Such a display of childish affection clearly bored Suzanne, and she turned her back on them. Her gaze fell upon Peter and Daisy. Peter, she ignored. She already knew what to expect from him. When her eyes fell on Daisy, they registered surprise. Julie Jones momentarily felt discovered, but she soon recognized the disdain that permeated Suzanne's appraising inspection.

Mrs. Hudson evaluated the new female. She had expected her stepdaughters, but she was obviously surprised to find an unfamiliar rival. Suzanne did not trust any of her own gender; all women were rivals. It was her nature to size up the competition immediately.

One quick glance told her that this female hovering beside the wonderfully attractive Peter was an inferior specimen, of no consequence. Daisy could read the contempt in her eyes.

Daisy, instead of being offended, relaxed

under the survey of the scornfully superior Mrs. Hudson. Suzanne did not recognize her former schoolmate and wouldn't be bothered with this "no-account." Daisy was glad to be thought a no-account. She would not have to do anything for this lady's benefit except stay out of her way.

Ray Hudson turned to his son, and they exchanged a hearty hug, somewhat awkwardly since Tabitha still clung to her grandpa's neck.

"Why, who's this little filly?" Ray inquired. Daisy saw Suzanne wince over the colloquialism, and Daisy felt a glimmer of amusement. The high-and-mighty obviously disliked her husband's willingness to pay attention to riffraff.

Peter put his arm around Daisy and pulled her close.

"This is Daisy Madden, Dad. She's the love of my life."

Daisy blushed.

"I'm pleased to meet you, Daisy," Ray said cordially. "This is my wife, Suzanne."

Suzanne audibly sighed.

"How do you do?" She arched her eyebrows, and a scene came back to Daisy's mind from her days at Madame Melanz's Conservatory.

One of the ten-year-old girls had heard

that the older girls were meeting in the cellar. She persuaded Julie to go with her and spy on them. They had hidden, and sure enough, four older girls had shown up and arranged themselves on the steps, closing the door to the first floor. Julie remembered stifling giggles as Suzanne had descended the steps theatrically and struck a match to a forbidden cigarette. She had then proceeded to promenade before the girls and spout off "wisdom" she had accumulated on men, marriage, wealth, and the running of private schools.

After the older girls had left, Julie and her chum had taken pencils and pretended they were cigarettes. They strutted back and forth in a fair imitation of their worldly wise upperclassman, mockingly imitating Suzanne's speech and facial expressions. It had been a hilarious afternoon at Suzanne Winthrop's expense.

Now clear, cold eyes examined Daisy from head to toe and came back to look in her face with undisguised disdain.

"Yes, I believe Lisa said you were a waitress." She paused for effect, then turned away. "How quaint."

A bubble of laughter rose to Daisy's throat and spilled over. "How quaint" was one of the phrases she and her friend had repeated over and over in imitation of Suzanne's sophistication.

Mrs. Hudson had not expected the girl she had snubbed to burst out in delighted laughter. Her head snapped around and her eyes narrowed as she looked at the impertinent girl.

"I'm sorry." Daisy knew an explanation was in order. "I heard someone say that in a sort of a play once. It was a put-on kind of production and terribly funny. I didn't realize people actually said, 'How quaint.' "

Peter cleared his throat. "Let me help you with the luggage, Dad. There are a couple of able-bodied men hiding in there. Tabby, go get your daddy and tell him his strong arms are needed."

Daisy took the cue to move on to other topics and asked, "You didn't drive from Florida. Isn't that where Lisa said you were?"

"Right," Ray said, relieved that the tense moment had passed. "We flew in to Corpus and drove down. I keep this car in a parking garage there."

"Was it a good trip?" Daisy asked politely.

"Coming home is always a good trip," Ray answered with feeling.

"Shall we discuss the weather next?" Suzanne cut in sarcastically.

Daisy remembered distinctly Suzanne's cutting remarks wounding tender hearts right and left at the conservatory. She sniped with her words, verbally abusing those less witty. Now, her words were not only rude, but they were playing havoc with a family Daisy cared about. Her own temper blazed. Before she made any effort to give the anger over to God, a cold retort formed in her mind.

She turned a mild and unassuming face to Suzanne's. "I don't think we could discuss the weather, Suzanne. It requires pleasantries, and you seem to be a few short."

Suzanne's sharp intake of breath indicated her displeasure, and everyone froze, waiting for her reaction. Daisy plunged ahead. "But you've come to the right place to pick up a few. Pleasantries, you know, kind words spoken for the benefit of someone other than oneself. This family overflows with consideration and kindness."

Joe and Mike shuffled out of the house, unaware they were entering a battlefield. Peter took the opportunity to grab a suitcase in one hand and Daisy's elbow in the other. He propelled her to the house. Once inside, they met up with Lisa. He pushed Daisy at the surprised Lisa and said, "Here, hide her from the vampire for awhile. Show her the house. Better yet, show her the barns. Keep her out of sight."

He turned on his heel and went back outside.

Lisa guided Daisy quickly down the hall and toward the back of the house.

"What on earth happened?" she asked.

"How could that woman embarrass your wonderful father like that?" Daisy fumed. "She's just a spoiled brat."

"That's the truth. Did she have her fangs out?"

"She's rude. A five year old has better manners."

"Some five year olds, Daisy. I've seen Tabitha display some mighty fierce temper tantrums."

"And I bet she gets spanked for them."

Lisa laughed as she pushed Daisy out the back door.

"You bet she does."

"Maybe Suzanne would benefit from similar instruction," Daisy said emphatically.

That sent Lisa off in a peal of laughter. "I can just see the scene with Dad and that old wooden spoon he used to use on us."

They stopped inside the first barn, which was empty save for some old farm equipment.

"Seriously, Daisy," Lisa began, "we try hard not to ruffle her feathers. I think Dad is very sorry he ever gave her his name, but he never says so. He's too much of a gentleman. Our mom was an extra special lady, and going by her instruction, we try to kill her with kindness. You know. Turn the other cheek. Heap coals upon her head. She hates being with us. I think it's because we're so good to her, it makes her feel rotten."

"I read in a book once that God gave us the law so that we could measure ourselves against it to see how far we fall short. Does that mean that by showing her how one should behave, you are making her look at how badly she behaves?"

"Yeah, in Suzanne's case we can always hope she'll start measuring. Personally, I'm more like Jonah, not wanting the Ninevites to repent. But my mom would want me to be nice to the woman out of respect to my dad."

"I really blew it, didn't I?" asked Daisy.

"I wasn't there, remember?" Lisa smiled warmly at her new friend. "You might not have paused to let God in on the conversation. Mom used to say that counting to ten wasn't good enough. We were supposed to count to five, 'One, God loves me. Two, God loves you. Three, God help me. Four, open my heart. Five, give me Your love.' It works most of the time."

"Most of the time?" Daisy tilted her head to one side.

Lisa laughed. "I had trouble counting past four when I was a younger Christian. It takes practice, and I don't think we ever have it down pat."

They found Bobby in the second barn talking to one of the horses.

"I'd sure like to ride one." Bobby perched on the top rail of the stall and stroked the face of the roan horse he visited. The horse pushed forward, almost knocking the young visitor off the board.

"Hold on, Bobby," said Lisa enthusiastically. "He's doing that because he's enjoying your company and he probably would like to go out just as much as you would. I don't see any reason why we can't go riding. Daisy, do you ride?" She turned inquiring eyes to her charge. A glimmer of mischief brightened her eyes. "It'll keep you out of harm's way for awhile."

"Yes, I love to ride." Daisy's face broke

into a warm smile at the thought of being astride a horse again, but it fell almost immediately. "I've ridden mostly on English saddles. Actually, I haven't been on a horse at all for three years. My father taught me on a western saddle when I was very young," she admitted. "However, I'm game to try. I'll bet the worst that will happen is that I'll be too sore to walk tomorrow." Her face clouded again after the brief lightening of her mood. "Lisa, I haven't got the right clothes."

"No problem," assured Lisa. "You are about the same size as Midge, and I bet she has something."

"I'm not going to change in the barn, am I? Aren't I to be kept out of sight?"

"Are you in trouble?" asked Bobby.

"I was rude," admitted Daisy.

"I bet it was to Aunt Suzanne," observed Bobby wisely. "She wants me to call her AWWWWWnt, and I always forget. That's why I came out to the barn as soon as I saw she was here. The Bible says to flee temptation."

Lisa giggled, but she redirected the conversation. "When we were kids, we often changed in the barn. Mom didn't like us dragging in all the mud and grime, so she had this old trailer installed in the back of the barn. It was heated and had running water. Let's go see if it's too cold to change in."

Surprisingly, the chilly trailer only had a few cobwebs for them to knock down. Bobby ran off with a message to the house, to be delivered, if at all possible, without disturbing Aunt Suzanne.

Bobby nodded after receiving his tactfully worded instructions. The sharp kid didn't want his temperamental aunt interfering with the proposed horseback ride. He delivered his message with the adeptness of an espionage agent and reported back that many of the house party were going to join them. The atmosphere inside the house since Suzanne's arrival was conducive to outside activity.

In an hour, ten not-quite cowboys hit the trail. Some of the smaller cowboys perched before an adult on the quarter horses. The biting wind forced them to pull their wraps tightly around them. The weak winter sun did little to warm them, but the temperature hovered around forty degrees, and when the wind died down, they unbuttoned their coats.

The girls wanted a bonfire as they had often had in earlier years. Aunt Harry and their dad had volunteered to load up supplies and come along later in the jeep.

Daisy sat her horse like an old cowhand, despite the unfamiliar saddle. She had ridden as a child and had attended a riding school in Europe. Riding stables were often part and parcel of the private schools she had attended.

She gradually relaxed, allowing the rough beauty of the south Texas mesquite, yucca plants, and scrub brush to capture her attention. Nothing out here reminded her of Uncle Jacob's devious plots.

They went across country five miles to a draw protected from the wind. A stream ran through it, and a hollowed-out place collected the water from a small stream into a shallow pond.

Peter explained, "This is a favorite water hole. Keep a sharp lookout, Bobby, you might see deer or a bobcat. Of course, it's more likely that you'll just see more cattle."

Daisy didn't know if he was saying that to pique Bobby's interest or if truly some animals would show up.

"Just so long as there are no snakes," she stated firmly, "I'll be happy."

Peter laughed, "It's time for all good little rattlesnakes to be taking their winter nap."

"Is that meant to reassure me?" Daisy asked with a mocking tone of voice. "What about all the bad big rattlesnakes?"

"Rattlesnakes aren't really that big," said Bobby, entering into the fun of teasing a female. "Not when you think of a boa constrictor or an anaconda. Texas rattlesnakes rarely grow over fifteen feet." He cast a conspirator's grin at Peter.

"He's just saying that to get you rattled, Daisy," Peter said seriously. "I've personally never seen one over twelve feet long."

"Rattled, huh?" Daisy grinned. "You couldn't resist that terrible pun. Totally ruined your credibility."

Peter grinned back, and for a moment they shared the intimacy of good friends sharing a bad joke. Bobby thought it looked pretty mushy and spurred his horse to catch up with better company.

He chose Lisa, and Daisy noted that Peter's sister welcomed the boy's companionship. Once they reached the spot chosen for the bonfire, they dismounted and went off to gather wood.

Daisy wondered how long it would be before Lisa and John would be able to adopt, and the thought spurred a question.

"Peter, why isn't Bobby with his parents?" she asked.

"His parents are divorced. He stays mainly with his dad, Uncle Henry's son. However, he's an engineer and his company sent him to Saudi Arabia. He could be there two years and Robert, Bobby's dad, says it's too tough for an American kid without a mother."

"So, he's staying with your uncle and aunt?"

"Yes, but that's not entirely satisfactory, either. They are doting grandparents, and on the one hand, they don't discipline enough, and on the other, they're too old to enjoy doing eight-year-old activities constantly."

"Why can't he stay with Lisa and John?" Daisy suggested.

Peter looked at her curiously. Turning his head, he looked over to where Lisa and Bobby were piling sticks, joking with John over the quality of work being done. A dispute arose as to whether size was a true measure of ability. They happily laughed over a lot of nonsense.

Peter took Daisy in his arms. "Just today I informed Uncle Henry that you certainly are not dumb."

Daisy's face assumed an expression of astonishment. "You mean to say that dear Uncle Henry said I am dumb?"

Peter laughed. "No, don't go charging after the poor old gentleman. The context of the conversation saves him from any blame."

"I guess I should be grateful that no matter what the context, you leapt to my defense."

"Having appointed myself dragon-slayer and knight in shining armor on your behalf since the day I met you, I am now willing to state that I shall always leap to your defense in any situation that threatens you."

He drew her closer and kissed her.

Chapter 15

Peter and Daisy walked away from the others.

"Uncle Henry mentioned that I should give you some time, that I'm rushing you." Peter sighed. "I'm old and rather settled in my way of thinking, and when I see something I want, I'm pretty sure of it. I know I want you to be my wife. I want to go on loving you forever, taking care of you and providing for you. He advised me to wait. See how good I am at taking my lawyer's advice?"

"Twenty-nine isn't ancient," Daisy commented.

"The point is not how old I am, but how young you are."

"Twenty-one isn't that young," Daisy objected.

"The point is, I love you, but do you love me?"

This didn't sound like Peter. Peter was decisive. Now he was unsure and hesitant in his speech. He looked at her beseechingly.

"I'm the guy who came along when you really needed help. Now you're grateful and perhaps you've mistaken it for love. Or maybe you know you're not in love with me, but you're just too kind to hurt my feelings." He let out an exasperated groan. "Listen to me. I sound like a sixteen-year-old boy with his first girl."

"Peter," she said.

"What?"

"I love you."

He crushed her in his arms and kissed her. "You'd better mean it, Daisy. I'm never going to let you go. Marry me."

"I have to think."

"No." He kissed her again, trying to prevent any thought processes getting started. "Marry me," he demanded between kisses.

"Let me think, Peter." He let her go, and she took a quick step back. She stood looking at him for a minute. Then she sighed as if making a monumental decision. "First, I have to tell you the truth."

Peter nodded.

"My name's not Daisy Madden."

A quizzical smile played at the corner of his mouth. "I guessed," he said.

She smiled back at him.

"Must you stand so far away from me

while you tell me the truth?" he asked, his eyes bright with mischief.

"I'm within arm's reach," she responded with the same playful grin. "I'm not running away."

"But it's so much warmer when you stand closer."

"It's an amazingly warm evening for November," she countered.

"You look tired. Wouldn't you like to lean against me?"

"Peter," she exclaimed, "I'm trying to talk to you about something very serious."

"You're right," he apologized, but he could not quite banish the happy smile from his lips. "I'm sorry."

"Sure you are." Her expression clearly said she didn't believe him. Daisy looked away from him for a moment while she gathered her thoughts. Taking a deep breath, she began her explanation.

"My name is Julie Jones. When you found me, I was running away from the French Estate Private Hospital. It's for rich mentally ill patients."

Without batting an eye, he asked, "So why were you there? You're not mentally ill."

She glanced up at him, her eyes reflecting her gratitude at his faith in her.

"Because my uncle paid to have me locked up out of his way. I don't have a drunken father. My parents died in a plane crash when I was eight. My uncle runs the business, and I inherited the controlling interest. By having me proven mentally ill and incompetent, my uncle remained in control."

"Come here and let me kiss you."

She obeyed and walked into his arms. Peter kissed her.

"Now, I have to tell you the truth."

She looked up at him inquisitively.

"Don't be mad, but I've known all this for a very long time. I just wanted to know you trusted me enough to tell me yourself." He waited for her response. She was now looking down at the zipper of his coat, hiding her expression. She did not speak, and he could not wait any longer. "Are you angry with me?"

"No," she said, "but if you knew, how did you know? And do others know? How close am I to being caught?"

"Uncle Henry knows, and we are doing everything possible to keep you safe. We had a private detective search out the facts, and Uncle Henry is now working on getting evidence to lock the scoundrels away."

"Uncle Jacob?"

"We hope so. If we can't get him behind bars, you will at least have your fortune back, and he'll be ruined financially. With the loss of his money, he loses power. Without that power, you should be safe."

"Nobody else knows?"

"No, and if there is trouble and I can't help, get to Uncle Henry. I'll give you his phone number and address. Dad would help, too, if he's here. But he doesn't know a thing about it. I'll ask if he's planning to stick around. Or rather if Suzanne is planning to grace us with her presence. Right now, let's think about our plans. When can we get married?"

"I haven't said yes yet, Peter." Daisy kissed him lightly. "Give me some time."

Peter groaned, "All right. But I can't wait forever. Remember, I'm practically a senior citizen."

When they returned, the bonfire blazed. Everyone but Suzanne had come out in the jeep to join the horseback riders. Aunt Harry had brought hot dogs and their fixings, marshmallows for roasting, and hot chocolate. The sun sank below the western horizon and the air turned colder. Peter and Daisy drew close to the fire with the others.

Peter's dad played the guitar and they sat around the fire singing songs that Daisy had never heard before.

"Your education has certainly been neglected," Ray Hudson teased her. "My daughters were singing these standards of Americana when they were just grasshoppers in the hay."

Lisa came to her defense. "Don't be too hard on her, Dad. She rides well, and she cooks well, and she's earning her keep waitressing. Sounds like things you were always trying to get your daughters to do."

"She'll make some young man a good wife," Peter threw in.

"Big brother, are you trying to tell us something?" asked Midge.

"No, I'm still trying to tell Daisy something."

"Well, let us know when she gets the message," put in Scram.

They left late and rode back to the ranch house by a beautiful moon. Daisy got her clothes out of the trailer. When she had changed, Peter steered her past the house to his car.

"We aren't going to say good night?" asked Daisy.

"No, Suzanne is unpleasantly drunk. They don't need us in there."

Chapter 16

A week had passed since Thanksgiving Day. The morning sun graced blue skies, and the crisp air held the briskness of a northerly breeze. Daisy wrapped her coat close about her as she started down the street toward work. She hadn't had to go in for breakfast, but she was expected soon.

A car pulled up beside her and a voice called, "Daisy, get in."

She turned with a start and saw Suzanne at the wheel.

"Why?"

"Hurry, there's been an accident. I'm supposed to take you to Ray."

"Why Ray? Is he hurt?"

"No, it's Peter. Hurry up! I had a hard time finding the street. I don't know this town like the rest of them."

Daisy climbed into the car and anxiously asked, "What happened?"

"I really don't know. I woke up to hear Ray packing a bag. He said Peter had been in an accident. He had me get up to come get you and we're supposed to meet him."

"Where are we supposed to meet him? This isn't the way to the ranch or the hospital."

"The airport. It's out in the country."

"I didn't know there was an airport."

"Well, it hardly qualifies. It's got two hangars and an airstrip about three yards wide."

"But why are we going to the airport? Where is Peter? What's happened to Peter?"

"Don't get hysterical," Suzanne said sharply. "I told you I don't know. His car turned over last night. They flew him to Corpus. Ray wants you to go to Corpus with him. So I was sent to find you and bring you to Ray."

They pulled into the little airport, and Daisy spotted Peter's father right away.

"He's next to that plane." She pointed. Suzanne drove across the field to the plane.

Before she had a chance to turn off the motor, Daisy jumped from the car and ran to Ray.

"What happened? Please, tell me what happened?" Ray Hudson looked twenty years older. He was pale and his mouth was set in a grim frown. His normally cheerful eyes were red-rimmed and distant. "His car was found this morning. He

151

was trapped in it. Apparently, he'd been there most of the night.

"His injuries were too much for our local hospital. They stabilized him and flew him to Corpus. They are going to operate on his legs." Ray's voice broke and he dashed his hand across his eyes. "I've got this plane ready, Daisy. He's been calling your name. He's really hurt bad, really messed up. I don't know if they can save him."

Daisy laid a hand on his arm. There didn't seem to be any words she could say.

"We must get going." Ray turned to climb in the plane.

Daisy looked at the little Cessna. The plane her parents had died in had been just such a personal "bush hopper." Since her parents' death, Julie Jones had never ridden in anything smaller than a commercial airline. She scanned the length of the small craft from nose to tail and found it looked disturbingly fragile. But Peter had called her name. She climbed in.

Ray Hudson was their pilot, and soon they were in the air. Daisy prayed with each thrum of the powerful engine. She only stopped to listen to Ray.

"I called Lisa," the worried father stammered. "She was going to the hospital to meet the helicopter carrying Peter. There will be a taxi waiting for us at the airport. I don't know why we are hurrying. He'll be in surgery for hours."

"We're hurrying because we love him," Daisy stated flatly. "Perhaps to the medical people his injuries won't seem so dangerous as we think. They see trauma patients all the time and they do miraculous things." Daisy stared down at the miniature houses. "We can hope, can't we?" she murmured. Her words were drowned by the roar of the small engine. Realizing Ray couldn't hear her, she repeated her question in a shout.

"I don't know. They said at our hospital that they saw no head injury or damage to his back. He's cut up, but he lived because no main arteries were severed."

"That's something to hold on to. God has protected him so far. He's placed Peter in good hands, I'm sure."

Ray Hudson didn't seem to hear any of her comforting thoughts. He continued as if she had not spoken.

"His left arm is broken in two places and a rib or two as well. They don't know what kind of internal injuries they will find there. We do know his legs are in danger." Ray's voice caught on a sob. "If only he hadn't been out there for so long before they found him."

"Who found him?"

"A couple of the ranch hands. He was on the old river road. And that's strange. Why did he go down that road last night? Why was he out there? When did he leave you?"

"A little before eleven. He didn't say anything unusual. I just thought he was going home."

They were both quiet. After some time, Daisy spoke. "He'll tell us when he wakes up, Mr. Hudson."

Ray nodded but didn't say anything. The possibility was too real that his son might never wake up.

They reached the hospital to find that Peter was not yet in surgery. His condition after the transport had been precarious and he had stabilized just within the last hour. Also, they had had to wait for an orthopedic surgeon to come in.

Lisa and John were waiting for them in the hallway and filled them in on what had been going on.

"He calls for Daisy, but anything else he mumbles," said Lisa.

John tapped her on the shoulder and pointed down the hall.

"Here comes his doctor." He indicated the gentlman who was approaching them in green surgery scrubs.

He came directly to Daisy, who clung to Ray Hudson's arm without realizing it. "Would you be Daisy?"

She nodded.

"Come with me. I want you to speak to him before we put him under. He keeps fighting to consciousness and calling for you. I want him to be reassured that you are here."

Daisy wordlessly left the others and followed the tall, calm man back down the hallway.

"He looks a mess. His nose is broken, and he has many little cuts on his face. What you see will look awful, but it isn't the serious part of his injuries. Try to keep your voice calm. Tell him you're here and that he is going to have surgery, and you will be here when he wakes up. I'm not sure he will hear you, but I believe in giving my patients every extra edge they can get."

Even with the doctor's kind preparation, Daisy gasped when she saw Peter. His head wounds had been cleaned and stitched, but the black and purple bruises, the yellow stain of the antiseptic, and the dried blood across the black stitches combined in an awful visage. He was connected by tubes to oxygen and an IV. His heart rate was being monitored, and the machine's steady monotone blips added to the desperate atmosphere of the scene.

The doctor's arm braced and guided her between the nurses, technicians, and equipment to stand beside Peter. His unbroken arm lay exposed on the bed sheets.

"Go ahead and touch him. It's all right. Speak to him," encouraged the doctor.

Daisy gingerly took Peter's cold, limp hand. She leaned forward. "Peter, Peter." There was no response. She looked imploringly over her shoulder at the doctor. He patted her arm.

"Just talk to him," he instructed and left her side.

"Peter, it's Daisy. I'm here. It's going to be all right. You're going to have surgery. I'm going to be right here. When you wake up, I'll be right here. Peter, please hear me." She caught back a sob. He looked so little like the Peter who was strong and confident, decisive and generous. He was swollen and deathly pale where he wasn't battered with bruises. He looked weak, and Daisy wondered if he would ever open his eyes again, if he would ever smile at her again, or say her name.

"Peter." She continued to speak an endless stream of the same reassurances. At some point her words turned into prayer, and she asked God to intervene for the one she loved, to give him strength and heal him. She thanked God for Peter and the great blessing he had been in her life. She thanked Him for everything in her life that had led her to trust in Him. Her prayer dissolved into encouraging words just for Peter.

He stirred. "Daisy."

"I'm here, Peter," she answered, squeezing his hand. For a second she believed she felt an answering pressure on her hand. Surely, he must have heard her.

They took him away to the operating room.

She followed them as far as she could, and then when he went through the last double doors where she could not follow, she turned to find Ray Hudson behind her. He encircled her with his arms, and she sobbed against his shoulder.

A little after noon, Suzanne appeared in the surgery waiting room. She answered the surprised looks with her usual attitude.

"I wasn't about to stay in Dooley with the rest of the clan in Corpus. Ray darling, I'll go check us into the Sea Castle Hotel.

We'll obviously need a place to stay while we're here."

Ray nodded, and Suzanne exited. Daisy noted she hadn't even asked after Peter. It didn't matter.

John found cups of soup in the cafeteria and brought them up. Knowing they had no appetites, he encouraged them to sip the broth.

Periodically, a nurse came from surgery and gave them a progress report. The extent of damage to the legs was completely repairable. There was some nerve damage and months of therapy were likely, but Peter would not lose his legs or the use of them. The team of doctors felt confident that circulation would be unimpeded, and barring complications, they could expect slow, steady progress toward normalcy.

Finally, Peter was returned to an intensive care unit. Each of the members of his family present visited him briefly. He didn't respond to their presence, but they received a measure of comfort just seeing that he was breathing. They nominated Daisy to be the one who stayed with him. Her eyes filled with tears as she realized the generosity of this offer. Again, she felt that she was a part of this family.

Sitting in the huge recliner chair in the

corner of the room, she watched Peter's rhythmic breathing. The monitors blipped a steady reassurance that everything was well. Daisy prayed gratefully for this man and his family and for the doctors and nurses who had been there to make a difference. Her mind wandered through a conversation with God, counting her blessings, imploring Him to keep them close, expressing her adoration for His presence in her life until she fell asleep.

The next day they moved him to a regular private room, and close to noon, he began to stir. Daisy talked to him and listened to his mumbling. He wanted to be sure she was there and that she would not leave. She promised every time he asked.

When his eyes opened, she knew he recognized her. He slipped back into unconsciousness, but she praised God, knowing Peter was going to be all right.

Every time Peter awoke, he wanted to see her. The nurses brought in a cot, and Daisy camped in the corner of the room.

Lisa packed a suitcase for her. The brand-new clothes came from a quick trip to the discount superstore.

"I wasn't about to buy you things from the Goodwill, Daisy," Lisa teased. "I had an enormous amount of fun on this shopping spree, and you are not to feel guilty. Daddy handed me his credit card and ordered me to do it. You wouldn't want me to disobey my father, would you?"

Daisy looked down at her waitress uniform, which she had been wearing for fifty-two hours. She nodded numbly and reached out a hand to take the offered suitcase.

"Who's taking care of Sidney?" she asked. The problem had settled in her mind. In all the turmoil of the accident, this was a simple difficulty that popped up again and again, as if by resolving this minor problem, she would have more control over the circumstances.

"The housekeeper," answered Lisa.

Daisy nodded listlessly. She looked at the still figure in the bed. So many tubes seemed to run out from Peter. He would be pleased that someone was taking care of his dog.

The third day, Peter showed much improvement. Each time he awoke more lucid. He still insisted that Daisy be right there beside him, and he would awake agitated until he saw her or heard her voice. Ray, Lisa, and John visited and tried to give Daisy a break. But neither Daisy nor Peter would cooperate.

On the fifth day, Peter got the idea in his head that he must marry Daisy now. He asked Ray to arrange it.

"Peter." His father spoke calmly and reasonably. "There is no hurry. You are going to be all right. There's plenty of time for that when you're stronger. Daisy will be right here."

"No, Dad." Peter was cross and distraught. "There's something I can't remember. I know I was thinking about it while I was under the car, but I can't remember. I've got to tell Uncle Henry."

"Tell him what, Peter?"

"I don't know what," he snapped. "I've got to marry her, Dad. It's important."

Peter would not drop the subject and became more and more anxious as the day went on. While he was resting under the influence of the painkillers, Ray took Daisy aside.

"Daisy, do you intend to marry Peter?" he asked solemnly.

"Yes," was her simple reply.

"Would it upset you to marry him now instead of waiting? Perhaps we could calm Peter down by agreeing to start the wedding preparations. He is improving daily, and tomorrow he might be more reasonable."

Daisy looked at Peter's dad and saw the concern the father held for his son. This man loved Peter and was willing, as she was, to do the unreasonable until he was more rational. "Next time he wakes up," she said, "let's tell him we can do it just as soon as we get the details worked out."

Peter awoke pleading with his dad to get busy and fix things so he could marry Daisy. Ray agreed.

"She needs a blood test. She can do that in the hospital. I don't want her to leave the hospital," Peter commanded.

Daisy smiled. Here was a trace of the take-charge Peter who had rescued her in the middle of her escape.

"And get Uncle Henry here. I have to tell him something."

"What, Peter?" inquired his dad. "Tell me, and I'll call him and tell him right now."

"I can't remember." Peter's surly tone matched the scowl on his disfigured face, and Ray asked no further questions of his son.

"Daisy, I can't feel that this is right." Ray relaxed in the chair while Daisy lay stretched out on her cot. Peter slept, still heavily sedated most of the time. "My girls

162

all had big lovely weddings, and you're going to miss out on that. This is a one-time thing, and you ought to have your pretties to remember."

Daisy laughed outright. "Mr. Hudson, look at my groom."

Ray turned to survey his sleeping son. "I see your point, Daisy. He does look like a cross between *The Mummies Rise Tonight* and *Frankenstein*. In addition to those gruesome black eyes, he hasn't shaved in a week."

"Lisa said she'd pick out a pretty dress. I'm not upset about the ceremony. I just want to marry him. Maybe he'll believe I won't disappear if he sees his ring on my finger."

"I've gotten the rings, Daisy. Peter won't be able to wear his till the swelling goes down in his left hand."

"Is Uncle Henry coming?"

Ray nodded. "Peter can tell him the vitally important message he can't remember." He sighed at the mystery.

"Maybe when he sees Uncle Henry's face, it'll come to him."

On Peter's tenth day in the hospital, he was sufficiently alert to participate in his wedding. Uncle Henry had arrived to help them get the license, and the minister from their church in Dooley drove up to do the ceremony. Lisa had picked out a knee-length evening gown of cream satin with a lace cape draped across one shoulder and tight lacy cuffs. Rhinestones danced in the light as they nestled in the folds of the cape.

The nurses thought the whole idea was fantastically romantic and joined in the spirit, finding room for Daisy to dress. Lisa arranged her hair in a fancy French braid with ribbons and flowers intertwined with the locks of hair. John shaved the groom, but at Lisa's insistence, he took a before and after picture of her "noble big brother."

The vows were exchanged with all due respect to their meaning. Daisy leaned over to kiss the groom in his bed. They were husband and wife. Peter sighed his relief.

"Now," said Uncle Henry, "I am going to take the bride out to dinner."

The groom looked startled and opened his mouth to object.

"Peter," Uncle Henry cast a stern look at his favorite nephew, "you are to rest. Daisy will be escorted by the entire family, and we will bring her back to you safe and sound. You have kept her a virtual prisoner in this room for ten days."

"Uncle Henry." Peter's strained voice showed the weakness of his present state. His thinking was getting hazy from the excitement of the day. "There is something I must tell you. I was thinking about it under the car. It's important."

"Yes, Peter," his uncle said patiently. "You've told us that before. You will soon remember what it is and be able to get it off your mind. Rest now. Maybe you will dream of it and be able to tell me when we get back from dinner. Now, don't fret. Just rest."

Chapter 17

Peter's eyes popped open. The hospital room was dark except for the night-light beside the door to the hall. He could hear Daisy's steady breathing from the cot in the corner. He shifted slightly, trying to ease the ache in his hips. How many days had it been since the accident? Eleven? No, twelve. He turned his head to peer through the darkness at Daisy's sleeping form.

"Daisy," he called softly.

She stirred immediately and rose on one elbow. When she saw him awake, she tossed back the covers and quickly rose. She came to the right side of his bed, and he put his arm around her waist.

His own personal angel. The thought warmed him, and Peter thanked God for this blessing. His good hand held her, lest she evaporate like some vision.

"Do you need something?" she asked. "Do you want me to call the nurse?"

"What time is it?"

She looked at the clock. "Three-twenty."

"They won't give me anything for pain

for awhile yet. I'll be okay. Lie down with me and talk." He smiled. "My thinking is a bit mystic as it is. I probably should guard against overdoing the drugs, even though the doctors think I'm within the safety range."

"What do you mean?"

"I'm not quite sure you floated to my bedside, but you sure look like an angel to me. My lovely angel, sweet and kind."

"You're right," agreed Daisy with a grin, "you don't need to get any higher."

She eased herself onto the bed, careful not to jostle him, and stretched out slowly. Her head rested on his shoulder with his arm protectively down her back.

"You okay?" she whispered.

"Not exactly," he answered.

"Am I hurting you?"

"No." He enjoyed the feeling of having her close. He noticed how little room she had. "But you can't be comfortable."

"I'm happy even if I'm not comfortable."

"Daisy, why was I out on that road? Where was I going?"

"Nobody knows, Peter. When you left my place, I thought you were going home."

Peter was quiet for a time.

"I was going home. Something happened, and I can't quite put my finger on it. Help me remember."

"How?"

"Tell me what happened before I left you."

"We came home from the diner. You had me fix you a sandwich."

"What kind?"

"Pastrami with cheese and sauerkraut."

"A person should be able to remember that." There was a hint of amusement in his voice, and Daisy smiled in the dark.

"Daisy, I do remember. It was dripping and made a mess on your couch."

"Yes, and I said, 'Thanks a lot. Now, I'll be sleeping with the smell of sauerkraut.'"

"And you objected when I kissed you good night. You said I tasted like an old German. I wanted to know how many old Germans you'd been kissing."

"That's right," she encouraged him.

"Turn your face up here so I can kiss you."

Daisy obliged. He kissed her softly.

"This blasted broken nose ruins my style."

"I'm just glad you weren't turned topsy-turvy in that car. Then your head would have been smashed instead of your legs."

"I think if I wasn't on all this pain stuff, I

could think more clearly. There is something that I was thinking under the car that made perfect sense, and it was important, but it's escaped me."

"It'll come back in time."

"That's the problem, Daisy. It feels urgent, as if there isn't any time to waste."

"And it has to do with Uncle Henry?" she prodded.

"Not directly . . ." Peter concentrated, trying to capture the elusive thought. "I need to tell him because he could . . ."

She felt his body tense. She twisted her face up to see his expression.

"I remember. Daisy, call Uncle Henry."

"It's not even four yet, Peter."

"It's important. Call him and get him here."

"I will not, Peter! It can wait until six o'clock. It's waited twelve days, and two more hours won't hurt."

"What if I forget again?"

"Tell me, and I'll remember," she urged.

His arm tightened around her. "No," he said. "But I want Dad and Uncle Henry here as soon as possible in the morning." His lips brushed the top of her head. "I don't think you've ever defied me before."

"Defied you?" she asked, puzzled.

"Didn't you refuse to make one little phone call for me?"

She laughed softly. "I suppose in our married life there will be times I will argue with you. But it is only to give you a chance to refine your wisdom with the benefit of another point of view."

He laughed and then groaned as his muscles reacted in pain from the movement. In a minute, he rubbed his cheek against her hair.

"Julie, I love you."

"Peter, don't call me that. It's not safe," she objected.

"You're my wife now. I am going to keep you safe."

"I love you, Peter."

"It's mighty inconvenient to be bound up like this on your honeymoon," he complained.

"For our second honeymoon let's pick a more secluded resort and leave all the nurses behind."

"Good idea."

Peter's six-o'clock pain medicine helped him to cope not only with his discomfort, but his impatience as well. He would have his dad and uncle by his bed soon. Daisy called both men after six and woke each one with Peter's imperious summons. They arrived around seven-thirty, both anxious to hear what he had to say.

"Dad, I want you to walk Daisy around the hospital while I tell Uncle Henry. Then, after I get his advice, we'll let you two in on it."

"Peter, I want to know now." Julie stood by his bed with no indication that she would oblige and go for a walk.

"Who was it that said a few more hours wouldn't matter? Let me discuss it with Uncle Henry first and get his legal opinion."

She recognized the futility of trying to dissuade him and chose to graciously accept his decision. "I don't think it's fair, but I'll do it." She made a face at him that made him laugh. He winced.

"Dad, watch her."

"Yes, Son," his dad answered seriously, though he thought Peter had been suffering from melodramatics ever since his accident.

As they left, Uncle Henry pulled a chair close to the bed and sat down. He leaned forward, his elbows on his knees, his hands clasped together in a double fist on which he rested his chin. He was at attention and waiting.

Peter took a deep breath and began. "It wasn't an accident. When I got to my house that night, there was a car parked in the street. One man was in the car. Another man approached my car before I got out. He asked directions to Palacio Street. He was referring to a piece of paper in his hand, which he brought over to the car, and he reached through the window to show it to me. He jammed it in my face. It was not paper but cloth, soaked with chloroform or something like it.

"The next thing I knew, I was under the car and hurting." He paused. "Those men wanted to kill me. The only explanation is that Julie's uncle Jacob knows where Julie is and wanted me out of the way so he could get to her. With me out of the picture, there would be no one likely to investigate what happened to her."

"We'll notify the police immediately, Peter. Her esteemed uncle is lying in wait for his next opportunity, and I don't like it. We have enough evidence to draw the noose tight. And if we miss a few culprits because we've had to move more quickly than we wanted, at least we will have Daisy safe and those current inmates freed."

Peter nodded.

"Now, I'm going downtown," said the

lawyer. He had a gleam in his eye as if he were a fighter going into a fray. "When Ray and Daisy return, tell them the truth. Ray will be a worthy ally. Daisy must be on her guard. You might hint that she needs to guard you as well. I don't want her running off in the mistaken belief that she will be taking danger away from you. You're helpless, and someone needs to hold your hand."

Uncle Henry grinned at the look of indignation that flared across his nephew's countenance. "Come on, Boy," he chided, "tell me you're ready to take on a couple of hoodlums."

"Don't rub it in, Uncle Henry," Peter growled. "Don't you know how it goes against the grain to know anyone could walk in here and grab my girl? I could shout about it and nothing else."

"We've got it under control, Peter," Uncle Henry assured him. "Nobody's going to snatch her."

He left, and ten minutes later, Daisy and Ray returned.

"We've had a nice little walk," said his dad. "And we've decided to get the truth out of you, one way or another. What's going on, Son?"

"Sit down, Dad," Peter directed. "This is

going to be a bit involved. In fact, I really don't feel up to it. Julie, why don't you tell Dad everything about the Estate and your escape. When you get finished, I'll tell him about the accident."

Ray turned curious eyes to his daughter-in-law. "I take it your name is not Daisy. This is an interesting beginning."

Daisy began with her real name and how she was brought up. She even mentioned that she had briefly attended a school where Mrs. Hudson was also a student. Her account of her imprisonment in the Estate Private Hospital was factual. She did not elaborate on the three lonely, desperate years. When she got to her escape, her voice warmed with enthusiasm. It was an adventure worth telling, especially the entrance of Peter, her knight in shining armor. She glowed as she finished her part of the tale.

"God has been so good to me, Mr. Hudson. Through all the bad experiences, He gave me hope. He never left me, and then it all led to good. Without His guidance, I might never have met Peter. God is so good."

Ray shook his head in wonderment. "How can you say that? Look at the two of you. Peter is broken to pieces, and you're hiding from a thoroughly evil and powerful uncle."

"But are we alone? Even before I met Peter, I knew that God was watching out for me and guiding me."

"It seems to me you've been on your own for the most part. It's just coincidence that you crawled into the backseat of the right car."

"Then I'd say you are on the outside looking in," Julie responded truthfully.

"What does that mean?" Ray was taken aback.

"You aren't a Christian."

"Of course I'm a Christian. Do I look Jewish or Hindu?" The sarcasm that so often riddled his wife's comments touched his words.

"What makes you a Christian?" Julie asked.

"I was born in America and went to a church most of my life."

"What do you believe about Christ?"

"The same thing everybody does."

"I believe my sins would send me to hell, but Christ's death and resurrection gave Him the right to save me. My acceptance of His love gives me the right to go to heaven."

"Peter's mother used to talk about

heaven and hell. Pretty old-fashioned concepts, if you ask me."

Julie laughed. "You know, I think God is probably as old-fashioned as He is futuristic. Being eternal, He would kind of have to be."

"Where did you get your faith from, Daisy — I mean, Julie?"

"My mother," she answered directly. "She introduced me to God and Jesus at a very early age. In fact, I don't really remember a time when she didn't talk about Him and pray with me. When she died, I clung to the fact that both my parents had been close to God. Since they were with Him, I could stay close to them by staying close to Him.

"But it was on one of my trips in Europe that I responded to the gospel message. It has sustained me through many lonely times. I've learned a lot by studying God's Word, but I've learned more by witnessing in my own life how faithful He is."

"I'm sure I'll never understand what you are talking about."

"And I'm just as sure you would understand if you truly tried to find out. God is the rewarder of those who seek Him."

Ray gazed at her steadfastly. She met his look without flinching. In her heart, she prayed that her words had somehow been used by God to reach this man she had grown to love as Peter's father.

He turned abruptly away from her, and she knew he had taken in as much as he could for the moment. He chose to put it aside for now. She prayed that the Holy Spirit would draw him closer to the kingdom of God.

"Peter," said Ray. "Are you asleep?"

Peter stirred. "I guess I drifted off while Julie was talking about the Estate. It is so inconvenient to be incapacitated now."

"You promised to tell us about the accident," reminded his dad.

"It wasn't an accident. Someone was deliberately trying to remove me from the scene."

Ray's face went blank with disbelief, and then in quick succession he looked incredulous, sickened, and finally outraged.

"You say this was an attempted murder." His voice held an edge of steel that Julie had never heard before. She scarcely noticed as the full realization of what this meant dawned upon her.

She grabbed Peter's good hand and clung to it. "Peter, because of me?" Her voice was full of anguish.

Peter turned his attention to her, remembering his uncle's warning. "Yes, Julie, because they knew I would do anything to protect you, and if you disappeared, I'd hound them like a dog until I found you."

"It's because of me you're hurt." Still the magnitude of what he was saying enveloped her, causing her to sway under an overwhelming sense of guilt.

"A soldier goes out to war to protect his country but, more specifically, his loved ones. It was a call I would have answered had someone stated it. I would do anything to protect you, Julie. But now, I need you. Until I can get on my feet, I have to depend on you. Don't let me down."

"I won't, Peter," she whispered.

"Remember your promise?" he quizzed her seriously.

She nodded. "I won't ever leave without saying good-bye."

"You must never leave me, Julie. I couldn't make it without you."

Chapter 18

Uncle Henry returned with a detective and a police artist in tow. An additional policeman stationed himself outside the door.

Detective Lieutenant Brock looked gruff and hardened by years on the police force. Sergeant Tina Perez, the artist, was small and feminine with dark hair and happy, friendly eyes. The lieutenant's stout six-foot-four frame filled the room as he entered. Sandy hair strictly groomed to remain in place crowned his otherwise unkempt appearance. Perhaps the control he exercised over every strand of hair was overcompensation for his naturally disheveled figure. The sergeant quickly retired to a corner and was hardly noticeable as an occupant of the room where the lieutenant commanded attention.

Peter fought fatigue in order to answer the policeman's questions. He had not seen the man in the car at all. He was able to give a fairly accurate description of the car, since he had looked at it closely, trying to identify it as belonging to one of his friends. Also, he had looked closely at the man who had approached him, expecting to recognize the late visitor as a neighbor.

Julie listened as Peter described the scene, and again she shuddered to think that these men had attacked Peter because of her. They were vicious and her Peter could be dead. She praised God they had not succeeded in killing him.

Uncle Henry and the detective left, but the artist remained. For the rest of the day, Tina Perez sat with Peter, and when he was awake, they worked on getting an image on paper of the man Peter remembered.

At four o'clock, one of the nurses came in to check Peter's vital signs. The many days in the hospital had increased Peter and Julie's circle of friends. This nurse was Patty, a huge blond who had been divorced three times and was raising three sons by herself. She was interested in what the policewoman and Peter were doing.

"With a policeman posted outside your door, everyone on the floor is curious. Is it true that your accident was attempted murder?" Patty asked outright.

Peter nodded.

"What are you drawing?" she asked Tina.

"These are composite pictures. I have a notebook here with facial features in many different forms. We put them together until we come up with a sketch that looks like the man Mr. Hudson remembers," she explained politely.

"I've seen those in TV shows," said Patty who made no effort to conceal her curiosity. "May I look?"

Sergeant Perez handed over the latest sketch. The nurse took it with interest and stood gazing at it. A worried frown came across her face. She handed it back.

"Can you give him heavier eyebrows?"

Patty watched intently as Tina wordlessly complied. Watching over the artist's shoulder, the nurse nodded.

"His ears hang down more, kind of floppy, not attached. You know, this earlobe part." She pointed with a large finger.

Again, the artist sketched in the change.

The nurse nodded decisively.

"He's been here."

Sergeant Perez showed the changes to Peter. Peter grimly nodded his head in agreement. The ears and eyebrows looked more like what he remembered.

Immediately, Sergeant Perez arose and took the sketch to the man on duty outside, warning him that this man had been seen in the hospital. She then called her station and left a message for her superior.

"Is there anything else you can add to this picture?" she asked the nurse.

"No," Patty answered, "I don't think so."

"A detective will come to ask you some questions. Try to recall everything about this man. Where he was, what he was doing, even his attitude. I'm going to take this picture downtown and run it through our computer. I'm glad you came along when you did." She smiled as she gathered up her paraphernalia and left the room.

Peter looked over at Julie and saw that she was pale and upset. "Come here, Honey." He beckoned her with his free hand.

She came to him and clasped his one good hand in both of hers. Her eyes were wide with fear. "He's been here," she whispered.

Patty straightened her considerable frame and bristled like a mother hen threatened by an ill-mannered farm dog. "He's not going to get past our nurses and that policeman," she reassured Julie. "We think a lot of you two, and he's going to find we can be a very protective gang."

Peter smiled at the nurse. "I can just see

you attacking him with one of those long needles you stick in my hip."

"We've got 'em longer than that. He just better not mess with us." She stormed out of the room.

"I bet she's on the way to alert the troops." Peter grinned. He squeezed Julie's hand. "I've missed you today."

"I've been here all day."

"Ah, but I've gotten used to having you all to myself with no one else around. Today, I had to concentrate on something else, and all I really wanted to do was talk to you and think about our future."

"And sleep, Peter," she teased. "You still sleep more than anything."

"Yes, but when I sleep I dream of you." He became more serious. "I can see some improvement. I am getting better."

"I know you are. You are looking better all the time. Why, the bruises across your nose and eyes have faded to a nice greenish yellow. And the swelling went down enough that I can admire those devilish green eyes."

"Now don't be telling me how handsome I am. It only increases the frustration I feel, knowing how much you appreciate your handsome husband."

"How is that?"

"I want to make love to my wife." He gazed at her sweet face. "And," he continued, "I'm hungry for pizza."

Julie chortled, knowing he was trying to ease her tension. "Now I know where I rank."

"It's a compliment, my dear." Peter joked with her. "Ever since I was in high school, pizza has been very high on my list of priorities. I make a pizza from scratch that we shall one day enjoy."

"Peter, normal living seems so very far away," she sighed.

He removed his hand from hers and laid it against the side of her head, feeling the texture of her soft hair.

"Not so very far away. I promise, Honey. Things will come quickly to a head, and then all this will be behind us. Be strong and of good courage. The Lord our God is with us."

Two days passed with a policeman always guarding the door. Uncle Henry brought news that the Estate was being subjected to a thorough investigation. Outside doctors were reviewing the patient records and interviewing the staff and inmates. Dr. French had tried to disappear but had been arrested in Los Angeles in an airport. Jacob Jones, however, could not be located to answer questions concerning the hospitalization of his niece, Julie Jones.

"There's no question about your having to go back there," Uncle Henry told Julie, his smile confident. "They will be shut down for good."

"What about Uncle Jacob?"

"His spokesman says that he obviously had been duped by Dr. French, and he is very distraught that you have suffered. He is, however, out of the country on business and will gladly talk to the press and investigators as soon as he returns."

Julie was staring down into her lap, where her clasped hands revealed how anxious she was.

"I need your official permission to sue on your behalf." Uncle Henry spoke gently. "Your investments shall be returned to you, I am sure. Whether we can bring him up on criminal charges is still up in the air. I think when French cooperates, we'll have the evidence we need to get a full conviction."

Julie's eyes filled with tears, and she quickly dropped her head.

"What is it?" asked Peter.

Julie looked at him with pain and confusion in her eyes. "He's my father's brother.

He's the only family I had for thirteen years. He never loved me, never visited me, or had me to visit him. Yet I always thought of him as my uncle who at least cared enough about me to provide the very best education and all sorts of different vacations. I used to imagine that he was trapped in his office, buried in paperwork, and he would think, 'Where would I like to go to escape it all?' Then, he'd know he couldn't get away and would think, 'I'll send little Julie, instead. She can enjoy it for me.' I know it was just fantasy, but it was pleasant to think someone loved me even if it was in a distant way."

Uncle Henry put his arm around her shoulders. "You've got real family now. When you took on our Peter, you took on all of us from Tiger to Ray's queen Suzanne."

Julie leaned her head against his shoulder and he gave her a comforting hug.

"That reminds me," he continued. "I brought Bobby down here with me. It looks like I'm not going to be allowed to take him back. Lisa and John want to keep him until my son Robert comes home. Bobby is in seventh heaven."

"Oh, that's going to make Lisa so happy."

"I think it will work out just fine. And

your affairs are going to work out as well. I wish we could do something for Ray and Suzanne. Their problems defy solution. I could have kicked my brother's backside for bringing that cat home. And I'm sure he's regretted his folly many times over."

"All we can do is support him," sighed Peter.

"We can pray," Julie reminded them.

"But what do we pray for?" asked Uncle Henry bitterly. "I'd like to pray an avalanche on her head the next time she insists they go off to some fancy ski resort. However, I'd be guilt-ridden if that prayer were answered."

"There's only one thing that really changes people," Peter said solemnly. "Nothing is impossible for God. He could heal their hurts and restore their lives."

"I find it hard to imagine Suzanne listening to the gospel." Uncle Henry's tone was scornful.

"But Peter's dad did one day." Both men looked up at Julie's eager face. "Have you ever told him you're a Christian?"

Neither man answered.

"Well?" she insisted.

"No," said Peter. "I've always felt uncomfortable. He's supposed to advise me as to how to live my life. It didn't seem my place to guide him."

"Timothy was a younger man and he was used in the lives of others," said Uncle Henry. "Presumably, some of those under his authority were actually older than he. I can't cast stones, though, since I've avoided the subject myself when it comes to my little brother. I always figured he'd resent it, just as he did when we were growing up and I tried to tell him what to do."

"I think if you just talk about your faith instead of pushing to make it his faith, he'll be interested," Julie proclaimed.

"See, Uncle Henry," Peter beamed, "I told you she wasn't dumb."

Chapter 19

Three weeks passed before the doctors spoke of arrangements to move Peter to a rehabilitation hospital where he would begin therapy. Uncle Henry had returned to Dallas. Suzanne had gone on a shopping trip to New York City. Ray flew back to the ranch and happily took care of things as if he'd never retired.

Dr. French sat in jail waiting for trial. Several of his business associates were also arrested. Most of the staff at the private hospital were not involved. Dr. French had rotated his workers to keep them in the dark. The former patients were out in the world again, though all of them were receiving treatment for drug addiction or therapy just to be able to integrate into real society again.

Uncle Jacob had eluded the law. His wife claimed to have no information as to his whereabouts. The investments that rightfully belonged under Julie's administration were being returned uncontested. Uncle Henry busily worked on legal matters on her behalf.

No further attempts had been made on Peter's life. The police had a name for one of the suspects. He was Leonard Day, a man with a long history of bad dealings. It looked like Uncle Jacob had dropped out of sight to save his neck, and with no one to foot the bills and pay a handsome fee, the criminals were likely to lose interest and disappear.

Julie was reading a book one day when Patty came in with a round of medication for Peter. Julie glanced up, and they exchanged pleasantries about the weather and the few days that were left before Christmas.

Peter took the small paper cup that contained his pills from the nurse. He placed it in the hand that extended from his cast-covered arm. With his right hand, he reached for his glass of water. Patty grinned at his predicament but offered no help. Julie had to laugh as she watched a puzzled look come over his face. With the glass in his good hand, he couldn't hold the pills, nor could he bend the arm in the cast to bring the little paper cup to his mouth. She stood up to help him.

"Do you want me to hold the glass of water or the pills?" she asked.

"The pills," he answered.

Julie dumped them into her hand, and Peter looked at them quizzically.

"My pills are usually orange. Those are gray. Patty, would you check my chart and see if the doctor has changed my meds. He usually tells me everything and he didn't mention it."

Patty scowled, all her teasing vanished. She whisked the gray pills away and returned shortly with the familiar orange ones.

"Mr. Hudson, we didn't make a mistake. A switch was made. We don't have those gray pills in our supply. I gave them to the officer and he's called his boss. I'm sure glad you noticed the difference. No telling what they are, but I'll bet it's not good."

The nurse's prediction was accurate. When the reports came back from the police lab, it was determined that Peter would have been dead had he taken those pills.

Evidently Uncle Jacob had not given up.

Lieutenant Brock came barreling through the hospital door into Peter's room. His usually dour face was split by an incongruous smile. Julie remembered a gargoyle that she had seen on a European castle. The stone image had worn a similar broad smile showing a row of discolored teeth.

"Good news," he boomed. "Leonard Day has been picked up in Houston. So far he's denying everything right and left." The big cop shrugged eloquently. "Would be nice if we had a good set of fingerprints from the car. But some sharp cop down in your neck of the woods got a bug to be a detective and dusted Mrs. Hudson's old living quarters for prints. Bingo! His prints and the fingerprints of a Harry O'Neill were everywhere. Now, if we lay our hands on the second guy, we can play them against each other and get them to talk."

The policeman actually rubbed his hands in glee over the prospect. Julie grinned. Somehow, she was reminded of a little boy playing cops and robbers. The image superimposed over the rugged, formidable lieutenant made it almost impossible for her not to giggle. She pressed her lips firmly together. She didn't think the gentleman would appreciate her sense of humor.

Peter spoke up. "We will be moving to the Dolman Rehabilitation Hospital in a couple of days. I can't expect the local police to provide a bodyguard for me indefinitely. I'd like to hire off-duty officers to fill in, or do you have an idea of a guard service to employ?"

Lieutenant Brock puzzled over the question before answering.

"We have officers who need to pick up the extra money, but you'll find scheduling them is a nuisance. There are several reputable companies that provide guard service, but there you run across screening their employees. It would be awfully easy to slip in an assassin."

"I remember reading in the paper recently about an officer who was shot and would be laid up for six months," Julie interrupted.

"That was Officer Rodriguez," acknowledged Brock.

"Well, couldn't we hire him to organize the off-duty officers? He'd know which ones were available, and he could use the telephone, and do it from his home."

Lieutenant Brock considered the idea. "I'll call him and propose it. It would be good for him as well as you. He was very popular, and the guys would enjoy working with him." The gruff lieutenant nodded abruptly and added so softly that Julie and Peter almost didn't hear him, "Keep his spirits up, too."

The day came for the transfer. Peter went in an ambulance, and Lisa and Bobby came to help Julie collect all the things she had accumulated. It was the first time Julie had been out of the hospital since her wedding dinner. As they drove past the dingy winter beach, Lisa teased her about freedom and the taste of the outside world. She smiled shyly.

Bobby popped off, "We're forgetting she's an old pro at being locked up. She's been in a prison camp for three years."

"Oh, my goodness, Bobby," Julie gasped. "Where did you get that idea?"

"I read all the papers, and Grandpa told me some things after they had it on TV about the crooks being arrested." The boy showed his enthusiasm about the subject.

"Maybe I'd better tell you a little about it," Julie suggested. "Half-truths can be very misleading."

"Yeah," said Bobby. "Tell me."

"First, the French Estate Private Hospital was nothing like a prison camp. We were surrounded by luxury. My room was very elegant, but it included a closed-circuit camera so that I could be monitored while in my room. The food was top-notch cuisine. And there were gardens to walk in and a pool that was opened twice a day but heavily supervised. There was a grand piano in the living room where I played for hours, and there was a library of maybe three thousand books. We were not allowed to listen to radio or watch TV, but that was because it upset many patients."

"It was like a posh resort?" Bobby's eyes were full of doubt.

"Yes," answered Julie, "but it still was a very unhappy place."

"I don't think I'd like having a camera on me in my bedroom," said Bobby. He turned to Lisa. "I don't do anything bad. It's just kind of a creepy idea."

"I agree," Lisa answered.

"You see," continued Julie, "you weren't supposed to be yourself or think for yourself. God created us to be individuals with minds, and they tried to obliterate that gift from God. God in His infinite wisdom made us cherish our right to choose and make decisions.

"That's an important part of becoming a Christian. People aren't born Christians or automatically made Christians because they go to church. They have the opportunity to learn about God, decide He is wise and good, and choose to follow Him. It is part of our nature to want to make the decision instead of being forced or manipulated into it."

"So you were unhappy 'cause you couldn't follow God?" Bobby tried to understand.

"I couldn't follow Christ freely. Within those walls, there was very limited opportunity to serve Him, worship Him, or tell others about Him. However, I did learn I could do small things. Just being kind to others, playing the piano to His glory, encouraging someone with the Word of God were some of the things that came my way. And praise God, I still had my Bible by my bed. In fact, I'd like to have my Bible. I left it behind."

"Maybe Grandpa can get it for you," Bobby commented.

"Maybe he can," said Julie. "The hard part was not choosing my own clothes or dinnertime or going out to town. I felt very confined. Remember, I had traveled all over Europe and Asia and parts of Africa. I even went to Brazil once. I had rarely stayed anywhere more than six months and to be locked away was entirely different. I needed Jesus to comfort me and be my friend. I knew that He was with me."

"So that's why you didn't go crazy?" Bobby was very serious.

"That's why," Julie answered emphatically.

"Boy, does He stick by me like that?" asked Bobby.

"I have no idea, Bobby. That depends on if you're a Christian," Julie answered honestly.

"How do I know if I'm a Christian?" he asked.

Julie sent up a silent prayer that she would have the right words. "First, you have to know there is a God."

"Sure, there is. My dad's talked about Him ever since I was little. What else do I have to know?" asked Bobby impatiently.

"Next, you have to know who Jesus is."

"That's easy. He was born on Christmas and died on Easter."

"What did He do in between?" Julie asked.

"He grew up and did miracles," Bobby stated simply.

"And taught about God. He was able to do these things because He is God's only Son."

"Yeah," Bobby easily agreed.

"What did He do after He died?"

"Huh?" This was a strange question.

"What did Jesus do after He died?" Julie repeated.

"I don't know," he admitted.

"He got up from the grave and wasn't dead any longer. He did some more miracles. Lots of people saw Him. Then, He went up to heaven to do another kind of job for God the Father, and He left us behind to continue His ministry here on earth until He comes again."

"Okay."

"Now, tell me why He died on the cross, Bobby."

"Because there were some bad men who wanted Him dead, so they rigged up a fake trial and killed Him."

"But He was the Son of God, Bobby, and He could have gotten off that cross anytime He wanted."

"Really?"

"Yes."

"Then why didn't He?"

"Because He wanted to pay our debts for us so we could go to heaven."

"If I know this stuff, can I go to heaven?"

"Yes, and He promises us that we are then His special children and He will never leave us or forsake us here on earth."

"Why did it have to be just Him that could do it?"

"Because He is God's perfect Son who

never sinned. When He died, He took on all the sin of every believer."

"You believe all this, don't you?"

Julie nodded.

"And Cousin Peter?"

Julie nodded again.

"And you, Cousin Lisa?"

"Yes, Bobby, I believe." Lisa's soft voice firmly acknowledged her allegiance to God.

"What do I do? Do I have to sign a paper or something?"

"No, Bobby," Julie answered. "Just talk to God in your heart. Tell Him the things you've just figured out. Tell Him about your sins. You don't have to list them all. It is enough to agree with Him that you do wrong things. Thank Him for His Son, Jesus, and ask Him to be the most important friend in your life."

"Right now?"

"Right now is fine. Lisa and I will be quiet so you can think it out."

Silence filled the car, but three people were very involved in prayer.

Some time later, Bobby spoke up. "I think we should stop and get Cousin Peter a pizza. He's going to be tired after the move, and he likes pizza almost as much as I do. He took me to a pizza place in Dallas when he was visiting once, and I only ate one more piece than he did. I had to though, 'cause it was a contest."

Lisa gasped, "Bobby, didn't you do it?"

"Yeah, I won the contest," Bobby explained.

"Not that, Bobby," Lisa was astonished. "Didn't you talk to God?"

"Oh, yeah," said Bobby, "that was miles ago. Now I'm hungry. Can't we get the pizza?"

"Sure, we'll get the pizza. And we'll tell Cousin Peter it is in celebration of something and make him guess what," agreed Lisa.

"Celebration because I believe in Jesus?" Bobby asked in bewilderment.

"Yes," Lisa beamed. "It says in the Bible that the angels rejoice over every saved sinner. If they are going to party, we ought to, too."

Cousin Peter was too exhausted to be enthusiastic about pizza, and he didn't eat much for the rest of the day. However, the news of Bobby's decision delighted him, and he wanted to shake hands with one of the newest members of the Kingdom. He urged Bobby to write his dad as soon as he got home.

Bobby looked at him with big eyes.

"This is a big deal, isn't it, Cousin Peter?"

"Yes, Bobby, a very big deal. You're going to find that you will be curious about exactly what the Bible says and how Jesus would act in all sorts of situations. For the rest of your life, you are going to be seeing God working, while other people who don't know Him can't seem to see a thing."

"Doesn't everybody do this?"

"Sad to say, many people never see the light."

"You look awful," Bobby commented bluntly. "Do you feel good about God even when you feel so crummy?"

"Yes," answered Peter. "And when I think of how crummy I'd feel if I had to go through this without His help, it makes me sick to my stomach."

"Let's let Peter rest, Bobby," Lisa said. "You and I need to go home and fix a special dinner and celebrate with Cousin John."

"Why don't we go out for pizza?" he suggested with his mouth full of the pizza they'd brought along.

"Bobby, you'll turn into a pizza," Lisa laughed.

"Cool. Then I'd speak Italian." Bobby's eyes danced, and they all laughed.

Chapter 20

"I hear carolers," Peter said as he dipped his spoon in the mandatory red Jell-O on his dinner tray. "This hospital has the same menu as the other. I can't wait to get into our own place and have a bowl of your soup, maybe an omelet, and a homemade pizza, my homemade pizza."

"Soup, omelet, and pizza together?" Julie's eyes crinkled as she questioned her husband's choice of menu. He was often cranky these days and sometimes his humor struck her as amusing.

Peter ignored her comment and changed the subject back to the music in the halls.

"Is that a radio or are there really carolers out there?"

"It sounds like real singers," answered Julie. She got up from her own dinner tray and went to open the door to the hall. "What date is it, Peter?"

Peter picked up the menu beside his tray and looked at the handwritten number scratched in the corner.

"December 23. Christmas is the day after tomorrow!"

Julie came back to take his hand.

"I don't have anything for your Christmas present and I'll bet you don't have anything for me," she lamented.

"You're right about that. I suppose I could get Lisa to shop for me. We both know she'd get a kick out of yet another shopping trip."

Julie grinned. Shopping was never a burden to her sister-in-law.

"I can't believe I forgot," complained Peter.

"You have had other things on your mind."

The carolers stopped outside their door. They sang two songs for the benefit of the patients in the rooms nearby, and then with a cheerful "Merry Christmas," they moved down the hall.

"Why don't we wait?" suggested Julie. "We could have our gift exchange in a couple of months."

Peter pushed the tray away with his good arm. "Get in here," he ordered, pulling back the covers.

Julie closed the door and lay down next to Peter, doing her best not to bump him. She carefully snuggled against his good side.

He whispered into her hair, "Ten more days and they'll take this cast off my arm — then I'm going to hug my wife with both arms."

Julie giggled. "You'd better go slow, Mr. Hudson. There is still a lot of you that is temporarily out of commission."

"I'm going to be the best rehab patient they have ever had," Peter bragged. "I have real motivation to get all my abilities back in working order. Meanwhile, I should be grateful my darling wife is satisfied with broken-nose kisses and one-armed hugs, waiting for Christmas, and generally putting our life on hold."

"I'm happy, Peter. I want nothing more than to make you happy, too."

"Loving you makes me happy," he said.

"Loving you makes me happy," she repeated.

Peter's therapist's name was Kitty, a name that did not fit her personality at all. She was six-foot-three inches tall, without one particle of fat on her anywhere. Her long blond hair was an overdone mass of curls that she lassoed into a loose ponytail. She probably could have lifted two men Peter's size, and she had as much compassion as a drill sergeant in a marine boot camp. To accentuate the oddities of her character, she had an elaborate mask of makeup with three different shades of eye shadow highlighted with heavy black eyeliner and eyebrows.

Quickly assessing his progress so far, Kitty outlined the program before him. She liked his attitude and said so bluntly. She warned him that she was a bully by nature and fully enjoyed her job.

Her daily visits were swift and effectual. Peter groaned when he heard her coming down the hall, worked diligently for her, and groaned with relief when she departed. Sometimes Julie chose to take her walks during the sessions. She was too soft-hearted and wanted to brain the taskmaster, even though she was getting excellent results. On one of these walks she met Andrew Skye.

"You're Mrs. Hudson, aren't you?" asked a young man as he stopped before her.

Julie paused and looked at the man warily. He was wearing the blue garb of the therapist, the male version of Kitty's uniform.

"Do I know you?" she asked.

"No." He smiled easily, showing two charming dimples that added to his boyish good looks. "I'm Andrew Skye and I work with Kitty in the children's wing. She speaks very highly of your husband."

Julie nodded, not knowing exactly what she was supposed to say. The man was friendly, but Julie felt she had the right to be cautious these days.

"I've seen you in the gardens often," Andrew said, obviously not concerned by her reticence. "I imagine it's kind of rough being cooped up in rehab when you aren't the patient."

Julie smiled her acknowledgment of the unnecessary sympathy. True, she was often waiting for Peter, waiting for him to wake up, waiting for him to get through with some therapy. But she was contented to be here, to be Mrs. Hudson.

"Mrs. Hudson, do you swim?" he asked.

"Yes, like a fish, and I really enjoy it," answered Julie, for the first time showing some enthusiasm.

"You know there's an indoor swimming pool here that we use for therapy. There are two hours every afternoon when the patients and their families can use it."

"Yes, I just haven't taken advantage of that yet. Maybe when Peter reaches that stage of his therapy."

"I'd like to ask a favor of you," Andrew said. Julie's eyebrows rose in surprise.

"I'm working," he continued, "with a little girl who needs the water workouts. Usually, I have the mother sit in on the sessions and then it is up to her to repeat the exercises two or three times between my sessions. However, this lady is a real bimbo and deathly afraid of the water. It works against me to even have her anywhere nearby. If you could sit in on the sessions and take over her practice sessions, I'd appreciate it. The girl is ten and a honey to work with if her mother is out of sight. When Mom's around, she reverts to a basket case."

"I'd be willing to try," she answered. Suddenly the idea of interacting with a child and being of some use appealed to her. She admitted to herself that her days were long and rather empty. Of course, being with her husband was wonderful, but too often he was tired from his therapy and irritable. As a honeymoon, it left much to be desired. Perhaps if she had something to occupy her time, she would be better company for Peter.

When she explained to Peter and asked if she could go shopping for a bathing suit, he said, "Sounds all right to me, but you take the guard with you when you go to the mall."

"Yes, Sir." She smiled at his bossy tone.

True to the unfathomable mandates of marketing, the stores were in the midst of January winter coat sales while they stocked their floors with beach attire. Julie went with her escort, Officer Camp, to a nearby mall early in the day when the crowds of shoppers were likely to be thin.

Finding a swimsuit proved an easy task. She also purchased a knee-length purple terry cloth cover-up with matching beach towel. Then, her eye was caught by the coats on clearance, and the thought of her Goodwill coat urged her to browse through the racks of sale items.

Officer Camp patiently hung around as she tried on one coat after another. Shopping in Europe had been a lot different than this, and Julie thoroughly enjoyed herself in a genuine American mall.

"My shift is going to end before we get back, Mrs. Hudson," said Officer Camp many hours later. He privately blessed his own wife for the comparatively short shopping excursions she dragged him on. He had followed Mrs. Hudson up one side of the mall and down the other on all three levels.

"What?" said Julie, looking up from a selection of men's pajamas.

"We need to be heading back. It's getting late."

Julie looked at her wristwatch. "Oh my," she exclaimed, shocked that so much time had slipped by. "Peter will have my head." She grinned at the rather comical caricature of the long-suffering husband whose wife shops till she drops.

The reality she faced when she returned to Peter's room late in the afternoon in no way resembled the lighthearted mental picture she had formed.

Peter glowered, his eyebrows lowered to just above his squinted eyes. He watched without comment as Julie and Officer Camp loaded down the sofa with packages. The policeman took note of the husband's mood and quickly made himself scarce. As soon as the door closed behind him, Julie turned to Peter. Her face reflected confusion and anger.

"Why are you being so rude?" she asked. "Couldn't you have even said a few pleasant words to that man? What on earth is wrong?"

"Nothing's wrong." Peter bit into the words with a petulant tone. "I expected you to be gone an hour, maybe an hour and a half. After two hours, I began to worry. During the third hour, I tried to remind myself that you don't get to shop very often. I couldn't concentrate on my therapy exercises because I wondered where my wife was. For the last hour and a half I've been wondering who they would send to tell me about the terrible accident or the kidnapping or whatever."

"You were worried," Julie commented, some of the heat having gone out of her anger. She looked at him with narrowed eyes, contemplating how she felt about this rather ridiculous overreaction on her husband's part. It was good that he cared for her. Right? Then how come it felt bad to be harangued like this when she returned unharmed?

She walked over to the sofa and began rummaging through the packages, putting things away without even showing off the purchases.

The silence in the room became oppressive. Julie carefully avoided looking directly at the ogre in the bed. She came across the pajamas she had taken such pleasure in buying for her husband. He was being unreasonable, but she could have called. She sneaked a peek in the mirror and saw he was staring at the ceiling. He must be tired of being in the bed. She had relished being away from the hospital; lost in her own pleasure, she had never once thought he might be concerned for her safety. She turned slowly to offer him the gift and try to apologize for her lack of consideration.

"I'm sorry, Peter," she spoke softly. She moved over to put her hand on his arm.

"Julie," he whispered, still staring at the ceiling, "I thought you were dead."

"But I promised I wouldn't go away without saying good-bye," she reminded him.

Peter's head turned quickly. He frowned as his eyes searched her face until he saw the gleam of mischief in her own dark eyes.

"I suppose you would have told St. Peter you had an errand to run before you could go through the gates."

Her shoulders relaxed when she heard the light note in his voice. She sat on the edge of the bed and stroked his arm.

"If he had any authority to grant me a favor, I might." She stretched out beside him, carefully adjusting to fit at the side of his body without jostling him. She was getting pretty adept at this maneuver. She laid the pajama package on his stomach.

"I am sorry I was so inconsiderate. You know, I never had to report to anyone when I was off gallivanting around Europe.

When I was in school, we had free time and a curfew. There was a set time to be back in the dormitories. But on the excursions, there was only the paid companion who was always at my side. Officer Camp was just like my chaperones, although a good deal less bossy. He was just there while I shopped. I didn't relate to the here and now and the husband waiting for me. Forgive me?"

Peter's arm tightened around her. "I've been a bear lately. I know it. While I was fretting over your disappearance, convinced your uncle had spirited you away, I realized how much I snap at you and order you around. It would have served me right if you had decided to take off to get away from yet another oppressive tyrant."

Julie smiled and hugged him gingerly. Full hugs still caused him to wince, even though those ribs were almost healed.

"We've had a real fight, haven't we?" She seemed pleased.

"I'd say it was more of a misunderstanding," insisted Peter.

"No, Peter," she objected. "I was really mad. I was thinking about what to throw at you that wouldn't hurt you too badly."

"Okay. I was wishing I could get out of this bed on my own power so I could strangle you the moment you came through that door."

"I love you, Peter."

"I love you, too, but I think I've missed something in the natural progression of this conversation."

"Umm?"

"Shouldn't you still be fuming at me? I was acting like a pig."

"Yes, but when couples have a fight . . ."

"Misunderstanding," he interrupted.

"Fight," she insisted. "Then they make up. Let's just skip the rest of the fighting part and get right to the making up."

Peter groaned and kissed the top of her head. "Oh, God," he prayed loud enough for her to hear, "get me out of these clumsy leg casts soon."

Chapter 21

"Couldn't you have found a bathing suit that covered more of your body?" The petulant tone was back in Peter's voice and Julie wanted to throttle him. She picked up the purple cover-up and put it on, hoping that it would indeed cover up the offending garment.

"This bathing suit had more material in it than most of the ones I saw at the mall, Peter."

"I just don't like the idea of all those healthy males ogling my wife."

"I am going to the children's exercise class."

"I've got eyes in my head, Julie. Not all the therapists are women like Kitty. Some of them are very healthy young males."

"That's the second time you've emphasized 'healthy,' Peter. Would you get off the 'healthy' kick? You're getting better. I'm patiently waiting for you. I'm not going to fool around with some guy just because he's walking on two legs. Just because he's 'healthy.' "

"I'm not doubting you," Peter protested. "It's just that I suddenly see the virtue of those black bloomers and bulging blouses my great-granny wore to dip in the ocean. Why don't you promise me to get into the water quickly so those 'healthy' male therapists won't get an eyeful?"

She turned to do battle and brought herself up short as she saw the corner of his mouth twitch.

"You're teasing me," she accused.

"Well, yes and no. It is frustrating to be tantalized by seeing you in that lovely but skimpy swimming suit. I confess to having the urge to hide you in the closet until I'm able to walk beside you and glower hideous threats at any male who dares to appreciate your figure."

"Peter, you have to relax a little bit." Julie nervously twisted the beach towel in her hand. She looked up to see that Peter's face had returned to that forbidding scowl.

"When I came home from shopping, you said something about being an oppressive tyrant."

Peter was silent. Julie turned away, bravely plunging on but not brave enough to watch his face.

"Sometimes lately I feel very confined. I do want to escape. I want to escape this room. I want to get away from your bad moods."

Peter was still silent.

"I know you aren't grouchy on purpose." Her voice faded away. She waited for him to speak.

"Come here," he said quietly, after what seemed to her a very long moment. She turned to see he had his good hand stretched out to her. Quickly she came across the room to his bed and took the offered hand. He squeezed her fingers gently, but he didn't speak.

"I must not be any good at relationships," she stumbled on. "If you think about it, for thirteen years I haven't had any close ties to anyone. Maybe I just can't be a good wife. I just don't know how."

"That's ridiculous," barked Peter. Immediately his face changed from impatience to concern. He continued in a softer tone of voice. "Julie, you are the most loving individual I have ever met. I thank God for you every day. I love you and I am very sure of your love for me. Please put up with me. I'll try to do better."

The pleading in his voice took her by surprise. She gazed down at the lines of worry on his brow, and with her free hand, she reached out as if to smooth them away.

He pulled the hand he held up to his lips and kissed her palm.

"Julie, I love you."

She nodded, unable to speak past the lump in her throat.

"You are fully capable of giving me all the love I need, and I will try to be less of a tyrant. I think we need to include God more in the areas of our marriage that give us trouble. What do you say we spend some of these long evenings in a Bible study? Just you and me."

"Yes," Julie readily agreed, feeling again the rush of happiness that this man brought her.

"And, we could make it a habit to pray together."

She nodded again.

"Forgive me?" he asked.

She hurt him when she threw herself down on his chest, but he suppressed the "Oomph" and hugged her tightly with his good arm.

Harry O'Neill was apprehended in Galveston. Between the two suspects, the police came up with a full confession. Each one would reveal something additional, and then the police would use that to their advantage in questioning the other. The pity was that the arrested men had no idea who was the person behind their employment. They had dealt with a middleman. Now police were tracking this criminal.

Uncle Henry flew down to visit Peter and Julie.

"This is a more comfortable setup for Julie," he commented soon after he had walked into the room. The hospital catered to long-term recovery, and the room had the hospital bed for Peter and a regular bed for Julie, since often a parent or spouse would be in residence with the patient. There was also a couch and chair and small desk. Double glass doors opened up to a small patio and a walkway ran down to a central garden. When Peter could use a wheelchair, they would be able to go on walks. Now, Peter insisted she take a walk with each officer as he came on duty. He told her she was going to be pale and puny-looking unless she got out.

Uncle Henry's visit concerned Julie's business interests.

"You're going to need a full-time executive to replace Jacob Jones. That man had a lot of business sense, but no scruples. Some of his dealings bordered on criminal; most of them were ruthless and did damage to a lot of poor people. His methods earned him a rotten reputation and many old business associates harbor a great deal of justified resentment.

"I suggest we send out a letter clarifying the position of the new management. Also, I believe there are many cases where you can make restitution. It means your profits will be down this year and quite possibly for the next two years. But you have it within your ability to do it, and I don't feel right about just letting it slide."

"I agree," Julie readily answered. "What about a business manager?"

"I'm thinking Peter is the logical choice. This is the kind of business he enjoys. He's a good rancher, but his heart is not in it like his dad's. Now that Ray has had to go back to the ranch in order to keep things going, he's a new man. He sounds like he's ten years younger when I've spoken to him on the phone."

"Now you know," said Peter to Julie. "I married you to get controlling interest in your inheritance."

"That's very ignoble of you, but I think you proposed before you knew the extent of my wealth. For that matter, I don't know the whole of it."

Uncle Henry laughed. "I've been involved with it for weeks, and I'm just now beginning to realize what a monumental project we've gotten into."

"Do you really think I can handle it?" asked Peter.

"I have absolutely no doubt," affirmed his lawyer uncle. "I'm so sure, I brought the first set of papers for you to go over and analyze. There is nothing wrong with your mind except you get tired easily. This will give you something to concentrate on in between those torture sessions they call therapy."

"Thanks, Uncle Henry," joked Peter. "You always were a thoughtful relative."

When the cast came off his arm, Peter declared he was half of a new man. From the waist up, he was doing very well. His nose was healed, though tender to the touch. The discoloration, which had gone from black and purple to greenish yellow to yellowish tan, had now faded away to his natural coloring. He was accustomed to more sun, so he still looked pale, and the many little scars from the shattered glass still crisscrossed his skin, mostly across the forehead. The doctors said those would fade with time. Only two were very deep, and those were in the hairline. One doctor joked that he had come very close to being scalped. Julie did not think it was funny.

His broken and cracked ribs were healed and his left arm looked puny next to his strong right arm. Kitty was quick to instigate exercises on behalf of the weakened muscles. She smiled with delight when she came in and saw him unencumbered with plaster. He groaned at her obvious pleasure.

Two days later, they removed the leg casts and replaced them with casts that could be taken on and off with Velcro straps. This also heralded the beginning of his water exercises, which he enjoyed. Soon, Julie, Peter, and their new little friend Katie were spending several hours every afternoon in the pool with other patients and family members.

Although Katie thought Julie was great, she obviously had an overwhelming crush on Peter. He could get her to try almost anything, but most often he was caught up in his own exercises. He rarely bothered with Katie other than to nod when she clamored for his attention. Julie wanted to shake her single-minded husband.

Chapter 22

Peter sighed in exasperation as he looked at the briefcase sitting on the sofa across the room. Where was Julie? He was tired from his morning bout with Killer Kitty, but not tired enough to sleep. If he could go through those papers one more time, they could send them off to Uncle Henry's office with the revisions marked. He didn't want to bother a nurse just to come hand him a briefcase.

Peter reached for the TV remote and switched on the set. He surfed through all fifty-six cable channels and hit the OFF button in disgust.

Perhaps Julie was helping with Katie's exercises, which meant she was also in the company of Andrew Skye. Peter didn't like Andrew Skye. It seemed to Peter that Andrew Skye was just a little too friendly. Whoever heard of a therapist who constantly needed some other patient's wife as an assistant? Killer Kitty never brought in outside help, certainly not help who wasn't on the hospital staff.

Peter reached for the newspaper on the

bedside stand and succeeded in knocking it to the floor out of reach. He leaned back against the pillows and glared at the ceiling.

"I'll talk to You about this, God, but I'm warning You, I'm not in a very congenial mood. I'm tired of this whole business. Get me out of here. I'm doing my part. I've never worked so hard in all my life. If I'm supposed to be learning to be humble, I think we marked that one off with the first go-round on the bedpan.

"If we're working on patience, doesn't holding my tongue when that squeaky-clean Andrew Skye comes around winking at Julie and escorting her off to help fix Katie's hair with new pink ribbons count as monumental self-control? Give me a break. Where's the girl's mother? When did Julie become a hairdresser? What business is it of muscle-bulging Andrew if Katie has a new hairdo to cheer her up?

"And pardon me for mentioning it, but it does seem a little unfair to bless me with an extremely attractive wife and then handicap me so I can't enjoy loving her."

Peter heard laughter in the halls and his face hardened. Julie was returning, but she wasn't alone. The door opened, and Peter got a glimpse of Andrew Skye, blue-eyed, blond locks, with muscles straining the blue fabric of his therapist uniform. The man was a caricature of health and good-will. Peter grimaced and bit off the "bah humbug" that sprang to his lips.

"Thanks for your help, Julie." Andrew reached out and placed a hand on the arm of Peter's wife. "Katie's progress is as much from your encouragement and friendship as from my skill."

"I am proud of her," agreed Julie. "See you tonight."

She turned into the room with a smile on her face that faded when she saw Peter's expression.

"Katie took three steps today," she announced with forced cheerfulness. She saw the paper on the floor and came over to pick it up. She offered it to Peter, and when he didn't take it, laid it back on the bedside table.

"How was your session with Kitty?"

"I stood up from a chair, walked across the room on the crutches, and sat down in another chair," he reported without any enthusiasm.

"That's great, Peter," replied Julie.

"Would you hand me the briefcase?"

"Sure." Julie quickly retrieved it and gave it to Peter. He took it without comment and proceeded to immerse himself in the paperwork.

"Peter, I didn't do anything wrong."

He didn't look up from his papers. "I didn't say you did." Fact was, he was being very careful not to say anything.

"Would you like me to get you a soda from the machine?"

"No, thank you." He'd like her to get rid of the lecherous therapist. There was no use pretending that the man was friendly in any way other than as a single male stalking a vulnerable, beautiful female.

"Are you going to join us for a swim this afternoon?"

"Probably." At least then he could glower at the Adonis therapist.

"I think I'll get a soda." Julie grabbed her change purse and bolted out the door.

Peter groaned. He was being a complete fool, and he couldn't stop himself. He vowed when she came back in, he'd do better. He'd apologize again and try not to be such an overbearing clod. He used to pride himself in his expertise when he dealt with his sisters. Where was that skill now? Hadn't he handled this skittish filly with finesse before they were married? What had turned him into such a heavy-handed hombre? How could she love and respect a man who pored over the Scriptures with her in the evening and browbeat her during the day?

All of his good intentions came to naught. She didn't return until it was time to get into his wheelchair and go down the hall to where the mobile patients ate in a dining room.

Julie pushed him up to the table where Katie and her mother sat. Two other patients would share their table, a teenage boy who had been in a motorcycle wreck and Mr. Gonzales, a stroke victim. As was Julie's custom, she then joined the servers and returned to the table when all the patients had their meals before them.

"Have you already prayed?" she asked.

"We waited for you," said Katie.

"Thanks," she returned with a smile. They reached out to hold hands, and Peter bowed his head, knowing they expected him to give the grace.

"Father, for the bounty of food before us, we thank You. For the bounty of forgiveness we receive through Your Son, we thank You. For the bounty of love we experience through Your Holy Spirit, we thank You. Bless us and strengthen us through this food to do Your will, and through Your wisdom, create in us a desire to do Your will. In Jesus' name, we pray. Amen."

The others dropped hands to pick up their forks, but Peter held on to Julie's until she turned to look at him.

"I've been a boor again," he said quietly, only for her ears. "Forgive me?"

She smiled weakly and nodded, but without much enthusiasm. Peter was often unbearably caustic and then just as earnestly repentant. Julie was getting tired of it. Peter was aware that his apology had only been accepted in a halfhearted way.

Silently Peter prayed for a solution to his problem. *Lord, I am fully aware that I am the one causing all this trauma. Please give me direction. If nothing else, stop up my mouth, tie my hands, keep me from further alienating the woman I love.*

As Peter passed the basket of rolls to Katie, he noticed her cheerful smile. She really was an endearing child. Peter watched and listened as his wife and this young girl interacted. Truly they had a remarkable friendship. Perhaps it would be expedient to his own peace of mind and his relationship with his wife to join their friendship.

It was Julie's involvement with Katie that took her away from his side. Peter had been so immersed in his own therapy that he hadn't really paid much attention to Katie other than to grouse about the time Julie spent with her. Andrew Skye really wasn't the person Julie was interested in. Peter vowed to be more involved in his wife's interests.

Lisa and Bobby showed up right after lunch to join them in the pool during the free swim. Peter welcomed them enthusiastically and his sister tossed him a quizzical look.

In the water, Peter felt much more confident. Without the wheelchair or cumbersome crutches, he could move with relative freedom in the pool.

Julie immediately entered into a game with some children. Soon Peter would begin the exercises he had learned. Peter watched Julie, longing to reestablish the rapport they had once had. For just a moment, he lounged in the water with his sister. With his new awareness of just how self-centered he had become, Peter realized that he had never told Lisa how much he appreciated her taking the time to come visit.

"Thanks for bringing Bobby out and joining us, Lisa. Julie looks forward to your visits."

"Brother," Lisa looked at him askance, "this is the second time today you've surprised me by being aware of something other than your therapy. Have they begun mental health rehabilitation on you in addition to the physical?"

Peter laughed uneasily. "Do you think I need it?"

"I think most people who are going through intensive rehab may be a bit single-minded, but given your rather forceful personality and stubborn streak, you've outdone most."

"You want to spell that out in plain English, little sister?" Peter asked even though he feared forthright Lisa was about to confirm his suspicions.

"You asked for it." Lisa grinned. "You have become a boor, a self-centered boor. You speak abruptly to Julie and give commands without using that pretty little word 'please' that our mother drilled into us. I'd throw a bedpan at you."

Peter looked across the pool to where Julie was playing a beach-ball game with Katie, Bobby, and several other young patients.

"She truly is a gift from God," he murmured.

"Yes," agreed Lisa, "and you've been

treating her like your own personal slave."

Peter nodded his head, acknowledging the truth of his sister's words. He decided to join the game instead of repeating the water exercises Kitty had given him. With strong, powerful strokes, he swam to the circle of children and took a position directly across from his wife.

Julie looked startled to see him. Again he was aware that during these times he usually stuck to his self-imposed regimen of work. He avoided the social atmosphere and concentrated on doing even more to accomplish his goal of regaining total use of his legs. His therapy, his goals, his problems. Perhaps his single-mindedness had been to the detriment of his relationship with his wife.

She smiled at him now and he felt a lightheartedness fill his soul. There was more to life than therapy. Thank God there was more!

When the young players went off in different directions to new interests, Peter stayed by Julie. They swam leisurely back and forth across the pool, just enjoying each other's company and chatting about nothing in particular.

Two hours of free swim passed quickly, and soon the pool would be taken over by the scheduled therapy sessions. The patients were beginning to climb out. Julie noticed that Katie clung to the edge of the pool talking to another patient, Hannah, giggling over some of the exercises inflicted upon them by Kitty.

The rest of the afternoon went quickly with a visit from the pastor of Lisa's church. They ate with the crowd in the dining hall and stayed a little longer than usual. An older man was telling stories of his days in vaudeville. Peter felt he made great strides toward relaxing and enjoying his wife's company.

As soon as they got back to the room, Peter was immersed in the long ritual of getting ready to retire for the night. Finally, he was alone with his wife.

"Julie, come here," he called quietly.

Julie came out of their bathroom with a hairbrush in her hand and a guarded expression on her face. She expected Andrew to come by soon. Whatever Peter wanted, she didn't want to get involved right now.

"Yes?" She stood in the doorway, not coming to his side.

"Can we talk?" asked Peter.

"How about in the morning?" she countered.

Instead of the angry, petulant expression

she expected on Peter's face, he looked concerned.

"You're going someplace?"

"Only to the dining room. I'm meeting Andrew," she admitted.

Peter nodded, and his face looked so sad, she realized how much she hurt him by being distant.

"He's bringing some material on courses I could take," Julie explained. "He thinks I could be a therapist. He says I'm really good with Katie, and I could specialize on children."

"You want a career?" asked Peter carefully. He felt they had made some progress this afternoon and he didn't want to sound condemning or scornful. He didn't want to cause her to withdraw any further.

Julie remained quiet. She studied the hairbrush in her hand, turning it slowly as if she would find the answer hidden on it.

She sighed. "No, not really. I thought I could help more with your therapy, but I realize it would be two years before I would be of any use to you, and by then you will not need me. I thought you might be proud of me, less angry that I just sit around doing nothing."

"Angry with you?" he asked, incredulous.

She nodded.

"Oh, Julie, no!" He stretched out a hand, hoping she would come to him. After hesitating a moment, she did. He grasped her hand, eager to explain now that he had some inkling of what was going wrong between them. "I'm angry with myself for taking so long to regain my mobility. I'm angry with your uncle for what he did. I'm angry with the police for not getting enough evidence to throw your uncle behind bars. I'm angry with Uncle Henry for how slow the court process takes, as if he could hurry it up. I'm even angry with God for allowing all this to happen. But I'm not angry with you."

"You don't act angry with anyone but me, Peter."

"That's because I trust you. I don't pretend everything is all right when I'm with you. It's hard to explain, Julie, but you're the one that gets the brunt of my anger because you're the one I love."

Julie squeezed his hand and he pulled her down beside him.

"Let me hold you," he begged. She stretched out beside him in the familiar position that lately she had avoided.

"Lisa told me I was being a self-centered boor. I've had my focus on myself and my therapy. I don't even know anything about your little friend, Katie. Why is her mother so uptight?"

"The same fire that burned Katie's legs so severely killed her sister. The mother is convinced the whole thing was her fault. She's paranoid that something else will happen to Katie."

"Doesn't sound like she has any faith in the goodness of God."

"She doesn't have any faith at all. She's had to go through all this without the knowledge that God loves her and her family. She's bitter and fearful." Julie craned her neck to look up into Peter's face. "I know I should be witnessing to her, but I can only think of little things to say once in awhile. In the face of what she's been through, my words of comfort sound trite."

"But we know they aren't trite, Julie. Don't worry about having the right words to say. I'm sure she witnesses your gentleness and peace even if you aren't verbally spouting great doctrine. I believe God uses you just as you are. He's used you in my life. Even today."

"Even today?" she asked.

He nodded emphatically. "Today, God got my attention through you. He told me that I had made out my own list of priorities without regarding His will. I haven't been content with the state I've found myself in, and by concentrating on getting myself out of this state through my own efforts, I have risked losing a great gift He has given me."

"Gift?"

"You."

There was a knock on the door, and Julie sprang off the bed and to her feet just as it opened.

"Hi," said Andrew, beaming. "Did you forget our appointment, Julie?"

"No, she didn't forget." Peter thrust down the immediate annoyance he felt. He must behave with more charity. He continued in a friendly tone. "She just got delayed. But I'm interested in this project of my wife's. Could you stay here and talk it over? I'd like to hear more, and I'm afraid I've been so wrapped up in my own therapy that I've neglected making friends with my wife's friends. I intend to get to know you and Katie."

Peter smiled at his wife. Julie smiled back. Their eyes caught and held, and a new look of understanding passed between them. A sigh of relief escaped Peter before he turned to pay attention to the young therapist's brochures and magazine articles about a career in physical therapy.

Chapter 23

Tom Quidmore escorted Peter and Julie when they went out for a Valentine's Day date. Everything about the lighthearted police officer was thick. He was indubitably short and squat. His frame was solid. His neck was thick like a football player's. His torso was thick. His arms and thighs were thick. He looked like a human block in a uniform with curly, flaming red hair on top.

Tom regaled them with teasing banter as he escorted the finely dressed couple to his jalopy. He made much of the fact that he'd tried to borrow the chief's car, but he wasn't trusted with anyone's vehicle, since he held the record for busting up patrol cars.

"You will drive carefully?" asked Julie, rising to the bait.

"Like I was driving the king and queen of Spain, Ma'am," he answered with a twinkle in his eye.

Julie and Officer Quidmore maneuvered Peter into the backseat, and Tom stowed the wheelchair in the trunk. He opened and shut the door for Mrs. Hudson, putting on a chauffeur's attitude. He gabbled about society celebrities in Corpus Christi while he drove. At the hotel, he helped them out and had the valet park his tin heap. Upstairs in the restaurant, he suddenly melted into the background, where he kept an eagle eye out for any possible trouble.

Peter and Julie sat at a table by the window overlooking the water. They watched the lighted waves wash against the shore.

"Remember we walked along that beach a long time ago?" Peter took her hand and smiled at her.

"I remember. It was cold."

"You were lovely then in that horrendous coat, but you are a vision tonight."

Julie blushed under his praise.

"Let's talk about the future," Peter urged. "By March first, I intend to be released from Dolman."

"Oh, you do?" interrupted Julie with arched eyebrows.

"Yes, I do," said Peter with confidence. "I think that's a reasonable goal. However, I'll remember not to neglect my wife," he promised. "I'll have to go in for therapy, so going back to Dooley is out of the picture for awhile."

"So what are we going to do?"

"Lisa and John are moving to a bigger apartment, and I figure we could move into the same apartment complex."

"Have you already rented the place?" Julie asked, annoyed that he was making all these plans and consulting her after the fact.

"No, but Lisa has two for you to go look at."

The last statement brought Julie up short. She had assumed that he wasn't allowing her to be a part of the decision-making process. She was wrong. How often was she going to be guilty of jumping to the wrong conclusion and causing tension between them?

Peter had disappointed her by being demanding and bossy. She understood that these characteristics had been part of his personality before the accident and were the same, only intensified, during the stressful period of his recovery. Now she realized that not only would she have to be tolerant of this while he was vulnerable, but she would also have to guard against developing bad habits of reaction in herself. She decided she would address this present issue with a light attitude.

"When did you two scheme this up? I thought you were never out of my sight except for therapy sessions in the torture chamber of Killer Kitty."

"You forgot the times you go help with Katie's therapy," Peter reminded her. "Katie's going to be an outpatient herself before too long. She's come a long way. I'm right proud of her. And I'm proud of you."

Julie glowed with happiness.

"I think we ought to venture out as a group and go to church next Sunday. The church Lisa and John attend would be perfect for her. There are a lot of outgoing young people there."

"Okay," agreed Julie. "I see now that you've gotten out once, you will be a hard man to keep behind bars."

"That's right, Honey," Peter joked. "I've had my taste of freedom and I like it." At once, he was serious, squeezing the hand he still held. "You've been terrific, Julie. You don't complain about being so confined. At least you don't if I remember to behave decently. It must bother you a lot after your experience at the Estate."

"Peter, you idiot," she laughed. "It is not the same at all. In the Estate, I chafed to get out to live my life. In the hospital with you, my life was right there to live. You are my life."

"Someday it will be more than just me.

We are going to fill a ranch with little ranch hands."

Julie smiled at the prospect. She loved it when he said something particularly "cowboy" to make her laugh.

"But now let's consider the immediate future. You'll have to do some shopping to furnish the apartment."

"Okay," she agreed.

"Have you decided about those courses Andrew outlined?"

She nodded, and Peter held his breath while waiting for her answer. He had decided to support her in any decision she made.

"I would like to try it."

"Well then, that's another reason not to rush back to Dooley. You can take classes in Corpus."

The music had started and couples were moving to the dance floor.

"Next year, we'll be dancing, too," Peter promised.

When they were ready to leave, Officer Tom Quidmore appeared to take them home. He was obviously "on duty" until he had them loaded in the car, and they were on their way back to the hospital. Then he began his stream of cheery banter while Peter and Julie held hands in the backseat. Peter answered with an occasional comment, but the policeman didn't really need any help with his conversation. Peter put his arm around his wife's shoulders, and she cuddled up against him.

An hour later, Peter lay in the dark tucked into his hospital bed, listening to his lovely wife putter around in the bathroom.

"Julie?"

She came to the door and the light from behind her outlined her figure as she stood in a shimmery nightgown.

"Do you need something?"

"Oh, yes, Honey, most definitely."

"A drink?"

"No."

"Do you need to get up to go to the bathroom again?"

"No."

"Are you overtired? Do you need a pain-killer?"

"I don't seem to be tired at all, and what's bothering me can't be touched by a painkiller."

"Peter, I am not a mind reader," Julie retorted, annoyed that he seemed to be beating about the bush. "What do you want?"

"You."

"You mean . . ."

"Yes."

Julie stood stunned for a moment.

"Are you sure?" she asked, breathless.

"Honey, this might be a bit of an awkward seduction, but I'm a determined man, and you, my wife, are going to be seduced. Turn off that light and come here."

Julie smiled shyly and turned off the bathroom light. Sometimes she liked the way Peter bossed her around.

They moved into the apartment the weekend after March 1.

Peter took on more of Julie's business affairs. Visitors representing different industries under their control began to call. For the most part, these were pleasant encounters. The executives were happy to have someone more reasonable to deal with than the previous management. Those who were of the same mind as the departed Jacob Jones were being weeded out of the companies owned by Julie Jones Hudson. Uncle Henry was invaluable help and had generated a division in his firm of lawyers just to handle the business Julie's interests brought in.

Policemen continued to keep them company. The off-duty officers wore their uniforms and were with them twenty-four hours a day. All of the men were friendly, but none of them were actual friends. In the interest of performing their duty, they were aloof and alert. Involvement with the family could possibly distract them and cause them to miss a suspicious circumstance.

Peter and Julie had become familiar with them all and had favorite characters among the dozen men who stood guard over them. It was a part of their lives, and they ceased to think of it as anything but normal.

Spring began to make itself felt in the air one day in early April. Julie had had an extra officer that morning to go shopping with her. She'd stopped at a greenhouse and loaded up with plants, some for inside the apartment and some for the patio. This officer left about fifteen minutes before the guard in the apartment was to be relieved by the afternoon duty officer.

Julie bustled around the kitchen fixing lunch. When she realized that Officer Cranz was still there, she was puzzled.

"Weren't you supposed to be relieved at noon?" she asked.

"Yes, Ma'am, but Kroger is late."

"Do you need to go? I'm sure we can manage for a few minutes."

The officer grinned. "Mrs. Hudson, you

ought to know better than that. I'll wait ten more minutes and then call Rodriguez."

Julie returned to the kitchen. Minutes later she heard the doorbell ring.

"Sorry I'm late. I had a hard time finding the place," she heard a strange voice explaining.

"Who are you?" asked Cranz.

"I'm new. Kroger couldn't make it, so Rodriguez called me."

"What precinct are you from?"

"Third. Just started. I used to work in Houston. I'm hoping this smaller city will be an easier job."

The telephone rang and Julie left her eavesdropping to answer it.

"Hello?" she said into the receiver.

"Mrs. Hudson, this is Kroger. I've had car trouble and I'm suspicious. I've already phoned for a patrol car to come by your place and check things out. Now, don't let on it's me, but if you think something might be wrong there, just tell me Mr. Hudson can't come to the phone."

Julie felt the skin on the back of her neck crawl. She looked up to see both policemen watching her.

"Maybe later," she said, hoping her voice wouldn't crack. "Peter is resting and can't come to the phone."

"Okay, Mrs. Hudson," returned the reassuring voice of her well-known Officer Kroger. "If there is someone there who shouldn't be, I want you to tell me how many by saying one o'clock for one, two o'clock for two, and so on."

"You could call back at one o'clock," she answered.

"Is Cranz still there?"

"Yes," Julie sighed.

"In case he hasn't caught on, I want you to keep him there. Talk to him about anything, boating, fishing, flowers, anything. The backup unit is on its way. Try to act natural and keep out of reach of the suspect. Don't leave the apartment. There might be an accomplice outside waiting."

"Okay, I'll tell him as soon as he wakes up." Julie hung up the phone.

She started back to the kitchen and then stopped as if she remembered something.

"Bob," she addressed Officer Cranz, whose first name was Bill. "I'll get that recipe for your wife that you wanted." Officer Cranz was also single and enjoyed his bachelorhood immensely. "I've got a backup copy. If I can find it, I'll only take a few minutes. If I have to write it out, it will take longer. Have you got a minute to stay?" she asked. Did he understand a backup unit was coming?

"Sure, Julie," Cram answered, using her first name when he had never called her anything but Mrs. Hudson or ma'am.

He got the message, she was sure. Julie slipped into the bedroom to sit with Peter. She whispered to him what was going on, even though she knew that the impostor hadn't a chance of overhearing her from the next room.

"I'm going out there." Peter grabbed his crutches.

"You are not." Julie moved between him and the door. "Let them handle it. You'd be something extra for them to worry about when they grab him."

"You're saying I'd be in the way." His tone was angry. The truth was that he would be in the way, and he knew it.

"You stay here and protect me," Julie cried. "If that man gets past the police, who's going to help me?"

"You're good, Julie. That argument will keep me by your side, but I want you to know I recognize it for what it is."

She put her arms around him. He leaned against her slightly and put the arm still holding the crutch around her slender shoulders.

"I'm scared," she said against his shoulder.

"It'll be all right," he reassured.

They stood waiting and praying. Soon they heard the backup policemen arrive. Apparently, the impostor recognized he was outmaneuvered and did not resist arrest. A knock on the bedroom door told them it was all over. Officer Cranz called, "Come on out, folks."

Julie opened the door, and Peter followed her into the room. The policemen were just escorting the criminal in handcuffs out the front door.

"Sorry for the inconvenience." Bill Cranz grinned. "I got to tell you, Mrs. Hudson, you are one cool dame."

"Really! You should have seen me clinging to Peter in the bedroom. That was the longest few minutes I've ever been through."

Peter sniffed the air.

"Julie, I think you're burning lunch."

"Oh, bother." Julie rushed to the kitchen. "It's ruined," she called back.

"Good," Peter proclaimed. "Let's order pizza." He turned to Officer Cranz. "That is one of Julie's major failings. She never thinks to order pizza. I think it comes from being raised in Europe. She's always fixing these delicious, well-balanced meals with things like brussels sprouts and asparagus. Mind you, it is all delectable. But someday I'm going to get in that kitchen and make her a super-Hudson homemade pizza that will knock her socks off. Our children will bless the days old Dad enters the kitchen and takes over."

Cranz smiled at Peter's oratory on Julie and pizza, but something came to his mind and his face became serious.

"By the way —"

Peter held up his hand. "Don't tell me. Lieutenant Brock will be by this afternoon to take our statements."

Cranz grinned again. "Yes, Sir, that's right."

Chapter 24

"She's not coming back, Son," Ray told Peter as the men sat in the living room of the apartment. "I can't say that I blame her. She never was cut out to be a rancher's wife. I should have seen that before I married her."

Peter hung his head, looking at his hands, not knowing how to console his dad.

Ray went on. "She called last night and said she'd had it and was filing for divorce. Ever since I married her, I've felt like I betrayed the memory of your mom. I felt like I'd let you kids down, though you never once said anything. Not one of you blew up and told me what a chump I'd been. I guess that was your mother's training in you. With Suzanne, I constantly felt that I'd failed her. The only way to please her was to be someone I'm not. I tried, but I failed."

Peter prayed silently. His father needed comfort beyond what he could give.

"You know, your mother only asked one thing of me that I wouldn't give her. She wanted me to be an entirely different person, too. But she never made me feel like dirt. She always made me feel like the king in his palace, even though I was too stubborn to change the one thing she asked for. She wanted me to be a Christian. She raised our kids to be Christians. Just before she died, she asked me to join her in heaven." Ray's voice broke with emotion and he dashed his hand across his eyes.

"I can still see her soft, lovely face. Her voice was always so ladylike. She was always a lady, even when she was cooking for twenty cowhands, or scrubbing the floors, or thrashing one of you kids for being ornery. She wanted me to trust her Savior, and I told her it was nonsense. Even when she was dying, I was too stubborn to admit I needed her Savior."

Peter watched the agony his dad was going through and was at a loss as to how to help.

"I should have listened. These past five years have been hell, and all she wanted for me was heaven."

"It's not too late, Dad." Peter spoke softly.

"I'm afraid it is, Peter." He sighed. "I'm an old fool. What kind of a God would take in an old fool at the end of his life?"

"Jesus tells a parable that says our loving God will do just that. Sometimes I've resented the fact that the parable says those who come late will reap the same benefits as those who labored all their lives. But now that it could mean my own dad, I don't care that there appears to be an injustice. I rejoice that you can have it all, too."

"I know all the words, Peter. I've heard the gospel preached all my life, though I've tried to avoid it, resisted its call. Do you think if I pray after all these years of scoffing, He's going to hear me?"

"He'll hear you and believe you and forgive you and accept you. His Word promises you won't be rejected. He can't cast you aside without damaging His own character. He has to fulfill His promises. He can't help it."

"Peter, I can't do it. It is like having to go to the principal's office when you know you deserve to be expelled."

"Are you remembering the time I had to go to the office for painting the lockers purple?"

Ray nodded and grinned.

"I remember that you went with me. I don't think I could have gone down that

251

hall and opened the door if you hadn't been beside me."

"You were as guilty as they come. You bought the paint, and your fingernails were caked with the stuff. You even had a purple streak in your hair," Ray recalled.

"Would you like me to go with you before the throne of God?" Peter asked. "One of the verses in the Bible says that a child of God has the privilege of boldly coming before the throne. I am a child of God, and I'm willing to go with you."

Ray gazed into his son's earnest eyes. After a moment of silence, he nodded his head and slipped from the chair to his knees. He'd seen his wife kneel beside their bed and scoffed at her. Maybe that was why he felt his confession must be made on his knees. Peter knelt beside him.

"Father in heaven," Peter began. "Please comfort my father and give him peace in his heart. Help to loosen his tongue so that he can speak to You. His heart is heavy, Lord, from the burden of rejecting You for so long, but You have drawn him close. Help him to make that last step that will put him in Your kingdom for eternity." Peter fell silent. In the gathering dusk of the day, Ray Hudson finally came before his Maker and confessed his need for a Savior.

When Julie returned from grocery shopping with her cop in tow, she found Peter's cop standing in the hall.

"What's up?" she quizzed.

"Mr. Hudson has a visitor. It's his father, I think."

Julie rushed in to find the two men having coffee.

"Were we expecting you, Mr. Hudson?" she asked.

"I object," said the older Mr. Hudson. "You have been married to my son for five months. Surely you can call me something besides Mr. Hudson."

Julie laughed. "How about Mr. Greenjeans?"

"No." He laughed, too. "How about Dad?"

She put down her bag of groceries and hugged him.

"It would be my honor, Dad," she said. Then with mischief in her eye, she said, "Dad?"

"Yes?"

"Will you go get the rest of the groceries?"

"My honor," he answered with a bow.

Chapter 25

"This makes me nervous," said Aunt Harry as she drove up the highway toward Austin.

"Nothing is going to happen," assured Peter. "The troopers are just a precaution because we're state witnesses. They are escorting us as a mere formality. Nobody expects trouble."

"That's not what I mean," objected Aunt Harry. "Every time I look in the rearview mirror, I think I'm going to be pulled over for speeding." Her eyes once more checked the little mirror and once more she saw the trooper's car.

"Are you speeding?" asked Julie.

"Of course not. I wouldn't dare," answered the flustered driver.

Peter and Julie were expected to testify in the trial against Dr. French. Uncle Henry had assured Julie that it would not be an arduous ordeal. He was right.

The actual time spent on the witness stand for each was less than one hour. The hard part proved to be the reporters who were following the trial and made coming and going to the courthouse miserable. Peter, although up on crutches, could not move fast and that made them prime targets. They spent two days in Austin, and as soon as their testimony was complete, they left by airplane for Corpus.

Peter testified about where he had picked up Julie and her general condition. The lawyer was most interested in whether she had seemed mentally competent at that time. Peter had to phrase his answers carefully, since he had thought from day one that she was incapable of taking care of herself. He said she was obviously intelligent and had thoughtfully planned the details of her escape. He did not say what he thought of those plans. He said she was in a state of near exhaustion, but she had been reasonable to deal with. He did not say that she was like a lost puppy in need of tender loving care. He added that in the months since her escape, she had proven to be a very capable young woman.

Julie's brief testimony was damaging to Dr. French. Her lucid recollections and precise information clearly revealed that she had been the victim, not a patient, in the scheme.

When the Hudsons reached Corpus Christi, Peter returned to therapy three times a week. Katie was gone, though, having returned to her home in Houston. She wrote letters of going back to school. Her letters bubbled with excitement over the news of the trial she'd seen on TV and read in the papers. Julie wrote back and bullied Peter into writing a paragraph, knowing the little girl would be more interested in what Peter had to say.

Julie's business interests and Peter's therapy kept them busy for weeks until Peter announced he couldn't stand the city for another minute, and they were going to go to Dooley for the Fourth of July weekend, and they could have a fireworks display on the ranch like the ones he remembered from his childhood.

Bobby, Lisa, and John jumped at the chance to go along. The private police force that kept surveillance over Peter and Julie seemed a bit excessive on a weekend trip to the country. The Hudsons decided the holiday from Friday to Sunday could be spent without their armed guards. Peter was mobile now and they would stick close together, not giving anyone an opportunity for mischief.

Julie stopped at Lisa's apartment to go over plans for the trip.

"I've packed some snacks for the trip."

256

Bobby grinned as he set down a second brown paper grocery bag filled to the top.

Lisa looked at the two bags on her kitchen table and shook her head. Julie grinned in anticipation; how was Lisa going to handle Bobby's excess diplomatically?

"Bobby," Lisa objected, "it's only a two-hour drive to the ranch, and we'll probably stop at Dillon's Truck Stop for hamburgers."

"Hamburgers?" Bobby was skeptical "John doesn't like hamburgers."

"He likes these," insisted Lisa. "Haven't you ever been to Dillon's?"

Bobby shook his head.

"They have burgers this big." Lisa held her hands out, indicating a circle as big as a dinner plate, and Bobby's eyes grew big as he imagined the size. "They claim to be the most famous hamburgers in the state, the biggest in the country, and the best in the world. You can also have venison hamburger, buffalo hamburger, or a weird thing they claim is a seaweed hamburger."

Bobby was intrigued by the prospect. "Well . . ." He considered the bag of junk food. "We'll probably need this stuff at Uncle Ray's," he pointed out practically. "You know when we were there at

Thanksgiving, there was nothing but rice and powdered milk in the cupboards. And the refrigerator wasn't even turned on."

"You're right," Julie chipped in, "but remember that your uncle Ray has been living there ever since, and he's stocked up by now."

"I wouldn't count on it. Dad took me hunting there once when I was real little, and we ate Vienna sausages more than anything else. There wasn't even any peanut butter." Bobby was close to pouting over the prospect of eating canned meat for a whole weekend.

Lisa thought about what she knew of her dad's eating habits after her mom had died. "You know what, Bobby? I think you have a point. I wonder how much of this stuff we can get in the car and still squeeze in us and the luggage."

Bobby brightened. "You're going to take my stuff?"

"Sure, but let's trade some of these chips for cans of soup, a loaf of bread, a jar of peanut butter, and jelly," Lisa suggested.

"How about breakfast?" Bobby asked. "We might go fishing, but if we don't catch anything . . ."

"I know he has cereal," said Julie.

"Yeah," agreed Bobby with no enthusiasm. "Nature stuff that tastes like straw."

Julie laughed out loud.

Lisa cast her a warning look.

"Hey, I'm sorry," she said, "but I don't like straw for breakfast, either!"

"You win," conceded Lisa. "Get a box of ours. We don't want you to turn into one of his cows."

"What is all this junk?" asked John in disbelief when they picked him up from the school where he worked. The others were already in the minivan and they were on their way out of town.

"This isn't junk," said Bobby.

"Yeah," said Lisa defensively. "This is selective stuff. Bobby, Julie, and I spent a lot of time deciding just what should come and what would be left behind."

John climbed into the driver's seat as Lisa moved over. "Did you bring the kitchen sink?"

"No, we had to take it out in order to fit in your fishing gear," she answered smartly.

"I thought," said Peter, "that they had packed for a week-long camping trip in Mexico. But they assured me we are going no farther south than the ranch."

"You guys have no right to fuss," complained Lisa. "We did all the work. Right, Bobby?"

"Right!" he answered with gusto.

Lisa turned to her sister-in-law. "Right, Julie?"

"Right," she said. She unexpectedly leaned over and gave Peter a bear hug.

Peter was surprised. "What was that for?"

"I just love your family." She grinned. Peter shook his head in amazement. They seemed pretty ordinary to him.

They reached the truck stop after dark. Bobby eagerly went inside and scrambled into a huge corner booth. He grabbed the menu and gasped when he saw that there was nothing but hamburgers to order on the main-dish column. The establishment boasted of Texas burgers for visitors, which were one-quarter pounders, hamburgers for moderate Texans, which were one-half pounders, and hamburgers for Real Texans that contained a pound of meat on a gigantic handmade bun. Lisa and Julie ordered the hamburgers for visitors. But the three men, Bobby included, ordered the Real Texan burger. The adults were skeptical as to the wisdom of Bobby's order, but not only did Bobby polish it off, he finished before anyone else.

He sat quietly, not interested in the

grown-ups' talk, until he began to feel very sleepy.

Julie saw him nodding. "You want to go for a walk with me before we get back in the car?" she asked.

"Sure." Bobby jumped at the chance.

"We'll stay close to the building," Julie told the others, and she and Bobby made good their escape.

They looked at the giant rigs and read some of the names the truck drivers had written on their cabs. A shiny blue one named Heaven's Sent and a red one with gray stripes named George's Buggy sat side by side. There was Spike's Speeder and Simon's Speeder. Julie and Bobby wondered if the two were related.

"What's that noise?" asked Bobby, tilting his head to hear better.

"I don't hear anything," remarked Julie.

"Listen," ordered Bobby.

She heard it then. A puppy was whimpering behind one of the semi-trucks. It yipped as if in pain.

"It's stuck or something." Bobby started around the dark corner.

"Wait, Bobby. We should get the others." But Bobby had already charged off. Julie followed. Around the corner, a little brown puppy pulled at a rope tied to a stake. He wriggled with ecstasy when he saw potential rescuers.

"It's all right, Bobby," said Julie. "Some trucker has tied him while he went in to eat. The puppy is just lonely, not hurt."

Bobby sat on the ground next to the furry, squirming mass of energy. "Isn't he great? I'll bet he's smart."

They jumped as a man came hurrying around the corner. "He's smart all right," he spoke loudly. "Would you like to have him? I thought I'd take him to my grandkids, but my daughter put her foot down when I showed up with the little tailwagger. No dog. Not now. Not ever."

"That's awful," exclaimed Bobby, truly distressed for the poor kids with such a mean mom. But the prospect of his getting their reject brought a smile to his face. "Can I go in and ask, Julie?"

"We'll both go in." Julie did not like the idea of waiting alone in the dark with this burly truck driver until the others came out.

Bobby began his plea before he even reached the table. To Julie's surprise, John got up and immediately went to investigate. By the time they had paid the bill and left the restaurant, Bobby was the proud owner of a born troublemaker. He had a sack of puppy food to squeeze into the car along with a water dish. John had paid a nominal amount to the driver.

"What are you going to name him?" asked Peter once they were on the road.

"I have to think about it," answered Bobby.

The puppy was wiggling to be free from Bobby's lap, eager to explore his new surroundings.

"I suggest Slugabed," said Julie, laughing at the puppy's antics. "He is obviously lacking in energy."

"How about Rasputin? He looks like a rascal," offered Peter.

Lisa said, "I like Cuddles. If he ever slows down, he'll be such a sweet little bundle to cuddle."

"Only his master will pick the right name," interrupted John. "You guys lay off Bobby and let him get acquainted with his dog."

The dog turned out to be a good traveler. Soon after the car was in motion, he settled on Bobby's lap and went to sleep.

Peter turned to his brother-in-law. "I didn't think you'd be such a pushover, John."

"Oh, Lisa and I have been talking about getting him a dog. We also think we might move to a house. Robert has called and said he would like to stay in Saudi indefinitely. Bobby will go spend a month or more with him this summer, but for most of the year, he'll be with us."

"Sounds like a great arrangement!" Peter was pleased.

Chapter 26

Ray, John, and Bobby shuffled around the ranch house kitchen at dawn.

Repeated invitations to those still in bed were ignored. The threesome stomped out for their early morning fishing expedition and brought back a string of fish several hours later.

"I caught the biggest fish," Bobby told Lisa.

"Hey, Buddy," interrupted John. "That's the only fish you caught. I caught the most."

Not to be outdone by this display of manly bragging, Ray put in his bit. "I may not have caught the biggest fish, but all of mine weighed more than John's. John would keep the babies in order to say he had the most."

John started to bluster, but Lisa stepped in. "John knows the smaller fish have the most tender meat."

Her father looked at her in dismay. "Girl, you don't believe that?"

Lisa grinned. "My own father used to

tell me the calves had tender meat. Veal, isn't it?"

"What applies to cattle doesn't necessarily apply to fish!"

"If you've cleaned those fish, I'll fry them," said Julie in an effort to divert the conversation. She thought the family was just being silly, but she wasn't quite sure. She was still getting used to their brand of bantering.

Lisa snatched the string of fish from her husband's hand. "They know better than to bring fish to the kitchen before they're cleaned. I'll fry, Julie, if you'll make the biscuits."

"Don't you remember I got a bad grade in pastries?" asked Julie, smiling. "Jesus turned a few fish into a feast for the multitude and my miracle is turning small bits of bread into stone."

Everyone laughed and they got on with the breakfast.

After they ate, Peter took Julie aside for a snuggle before she went horseback riding with the others. "Do you know what you did this morning?"

"Made chewable biscuits?"

"No, you joined in the jesting with my family. That's the first time you've done that." He kissed her. "You're beginning to feel comfortable with them."

"Yes, I am," Julie agreed, pleased with this little bit of evidence that she was really becoming part of her husband's family. She went off for her ride in great spirits.

After lunch, the family played cards until Peter lay down for a nap. Ray sorted through some papers he wanted to show Peter when he woke up, and John and Lisa went to visit some friends. Julie and Bobby went outside to play with the dog.

"I've decided to call him Higgins," said Bobby.

"He looks like a Higgins," said Julie, tilting her head and watching the puppy investigate a pile of rocks. "Where have you heard that name before?"

"There was a boy in my class named Josh Higgins at school a long time ago. He never could sit still in his chair and sometimes the teacher made him stand up 'cause he made so much noise shuffling his chair and the desk around."

Bobby abruptly called, "Hey, Higgins." The dog had taken off down the dirt road. "Come back!"

The little monster looked over his shoulder in a "catch me if you can" challenge and ran faster. Bobby took off after him. Julie followed in a leisurely way. She didn't see how anyone could run in the afternoon sun of a Texas July.

They had gone quite a ways down the road and were almost to the little bridge that forded a small stream.

"Can we go on to the brook?" Bobby called back to Julie.

"Sure," she answered and waved him on.

By the time she got there, Bobby and the puppy were splashing in the slow muddy waters.

"Watch out for water snakes," Julie warned and sat down on the bank under a scrubby mesquite tree, being careful to avoid the long thorns.

The boy and dog tirelessly splashed in and out of the water. Julie figured any snake with an ounce of self-preservation was miles away by now. No breeze moved the hot air. At the Estate she would have spent much of the afternoon in the pool. She thought it would be nice to have a pool when she and Peter settled down after the therapy sessions were over. Perhaps in the backyard of his house in town. She smiled as she imagined him teaching their children to swim much as her father had taught her. She pulled vague memories of her laughing, carefree father from the depths of her mind.

"Julie." Bobby's frantic call brought her out of her musings. "Higgins took off."

Julie jumped to her feet, and the two humans began pursuit of the exasperating puppy.

Bobby scooped tired Higgins into his arms. The dog's long pink tongue hung out as he panted. He had finally stopped scampering just out of their reach and lay down in a little spot of shade.

"You rascal," scolded Bobby. "You're bad. Bad dog!"

"Which way should we go?" asked Julie. The surrounding countryside looked forbidding. As far as they could see, short prickly bushes dotted the barren land. It all looked the same. Julie had no idea which way was east or west, and even if she figured it out from the position of the sun, she still didn't know in which direction the ranch house lay.

Bobby knew.

"See the low place over there?" He pointed and Julie focused on the horizon.

"No," she answered, dismayed.

"See that patch of green?" continued Bobby with patience. "That's treetops. The ground dips down and there is water there.

The trees grow and we can see the leafy green stuff on top but it looks like it is just short bushes. That's where we had the bonfire last Thanksgiving."

"You're sure?" It all looked pretty much the same to Julie, various shades of washed-out green with lots of brown and sandy tan.

"Yeah," answered Bobby confidently. "Uncle Ray used to take me out riding before he got married."

"Bobby, that was three years ago! You sure you remember?"

"Relax, Julie. He used to tell me it could be a matter of life or death to know what you were doing in this country. I paid attention."

"Okay," said Julie. "So where are we and which direction do we go?" Julie wasn't sure about relying on Bobby's store of knowledge, but his was bigger than hers, so she might as well trust in him while she sent prayers up to God that he was right.

Bobby sensed her skepticism and decided to show off.

"That's a teddy bear cholla." He pointed at a twelve-inch upright plant densely covered with yellowish gray spines so thick they looked like fuzz. His finger moved to another larger cactus that spread out with platter-type leaves frugally covered with large ugly spikes. "That's a prickly pear, and that's a hedge hog. It has water stored in the barrel."

"I'm impressed," Julie admitted. "So which way do we go?"

"The ranch house is over there."

They stood up and began to walk. Higgins ran ahead and looped back whenever Bobby called.

"Maybe he's learned his lesson," commented Bobby. "It's good to have him with us. If a snake sees him, it's more likely to slither off than challenge him."

"Snakes?"

"Rattlers."

"Bobby, this is not a good time to tease about snakes."

"I'm not teasing. Watch where you step."

Julie prayed again. Surely the God who turned a rod into a snake for Moses would be willing to turn rattlers away from their path.

They walked on in silence, trudging through the sparse underbrush. Higgins got tired and lay down in a small patch of shade under what Bobby said was a soapberry. Julie was too hot and tired to comment. Bobby picked up his puppy and trekked on.

How does he do it? wondered Julie. Her

back was wet with sweat. Her throat felt like she had swallowed cotton, and her feet hurt from stepping on rocks, since the soles of her shoes did little to protect her. Her legs weighed a ton and were gaining weight with every step.

"Bobby, I have to rest."

"We're almost there."

"I don't see the house."

"You won't till we get past the hill."

"The hill?" Julie looked out over the flat land and thought maybe Bobby shouldn't be trusted after all. She sunk down and sat without ceremony on the barren soil.

Bobby sat beside her and Higgins jumped out of his arms.

"You should at least sit in the shade."

Julie looked around. "What shade?"

"You're really sunburned."

A sarcastic answer came to Julie's mind, but she was too tired to express it. Besides, Bobby had been a real trooper. She was the whiner. At least she refrained from voicing much of her complaining. Julie brought her knees up and dropped her head down to rest.

"It's not a good idea to stay here," prompted Bobby.

"Just a minute, Bobby, just a minute," whispered Julie.

Bobby sighed.

"I'm tired, too. And thirsty. Really, Julie, it's not much farther."

Julie didn't answer.

"I could go ahead and get help and bring it back," Bobby offered.

Julie lifted her head and gave him a weak smile. "Bobby, you're the greatest. I'm coming."

They stood up and Bobby called to Higgins. He didn't come and Bobby called more urgently. Julie joined in. Had the puppy wandered off again?

"Higgins, Higgins," Bobby yelled.

There was a crashing noise in the underbrush. Higgins bounded through, closely followed by a low-slung, powerfully built basset.

"Sidney," exclaimed Bobby and Julie in unison.

"Where did you come from?" asked Julie as she bent to greet the dog.

"See," said Bobby, "we are close. Come on, Julie. I'm so thirsty, I could croak!"

Bobby started off with renewed vigor and Julie followed. The dogs bounced around their ankles, then darted off into the tangle of weeds and scrub and returned to urge them on. Soon Bobby had outdistanced Julie.

"We're almost to the top of the hill,"

Bobby called over his shoulder. "I see Peter. He's coming this way. Hurry up, Julie!"

Bobby ran on, and Julie watched as he disappeared over the horizon. There must have been an incline, she realized as she followed, hurrying now that she knew Peter was just ahead.

She was surprised to see the land drop away when she finally got to the high point. Looking back, she saw that the rise had been too gradual to notice. This was the crest of the "hill." Ahead of her, the ground slanted away, and she saw the dirt road coming off of the highway and the house and barns of the main house.

She caught sight of Bobby just as he reached Peter. Suddenly her strength was renewed and she scrambled down through the cactus.

He used a cane now, but knowing that he still toppled easily, she forced herself not to tackle him. He carried a sports bottle, and as soon as Bobby had taken a drink, he handed it to her.

"Peter, I've never been so glad to see anyone." She hugged him.

"I'm glad to see you, too, Honey, but we've got a problem."

"What?" Her face crumpled into a frown.

"Jacob Jones is at the house."

Chapter 27

"Uncle Jacob?" Julie squeaked.

"That's the bad guy, isn't it?" Bobby's eyes grew big.

"Yes," said Peter as he started herding them across the field. "Let me tell you real quick what has been going on. We need to act fast."

"Why are you pushing us away from the house?" asked Julie.

"We're not going in," answered Peter. "We're going to the barn. John and Lisa came back from town and they brought Sidney with them. I took Sidney out to look for you because I was getting worried. I saw a car I didn't recognize come up to the house and three men get out. I didn't have any luck finding you, so I turned back. When I got back to the house, I looked in the window just as I was passing by."

They had reached the barn, and Peter steered them to the back door.

"The men were all together in the front room. One of them held a gun and it was obviously not a cordial visit. That's when I recognized your uncle from pictures my uncle Henry had."

"He's in there with a gun!" Julie's voice came out in a squeaky whisper.

"No, he's just sitting there. It's one of his henchmen who has the gun."

"But your dad, John, and Lisa are in there with henchmen?"

Peter nodded.

"We've got to do something!"

"I'll ride for help on one of the horses," volunteered Bobby.

"No," said Peter, "but I am going to ask you to do something dangerous."

Julie frowned at Bobby's enthusiasm. This was serious.

"What? Do you want me to go in and distract them?"

"No, I want you to sneak in the back way, go up to Lisa's room, and bring back her cellular phone."

Bobby nodded. "Sure."

Julie shuddered and she took hold of his arm. "Bobby, this isn't a game. Those men are criminals."

"I'll be careful, Julie." He patted her hand. "You don't have to worry."

"I can't help but worry," Julie said emphatically.

"You should pray." When she didn't respond, he gave her a big hug and then pulled away. "Okay, here I go."

He slipped out before someone could make another objection and interfere with his adventure.

Peter and Julie stood facing each other in the dim light of the barn. Horses shuffled in their stalls. Higgins and Sidney sniffed around, enjoying the smells of hay and animals that drifted around them.

"I'm scared," said Julie.

"Come here." Peter held his arms open. She walked into them and laid her head against his chest.

"Pray, Peter, pray."

They stood together as Peter said a quick prayer of protection for Bobby as he sneaked through the house and for those who were sitting in the living room with the gunman.

"I'm back," Bobby announced as he came through the door. He held up the cellular.

Peter dialed, reported the situation succinctly, and hung up.

"They say sit tight," he said as he shut the unit. "Man, I don't like this. Somebody is going to get hurt." He rubbed his hand over his chin. "I'm going in."

"No!" said Julie.

"Julie," said Peter. "I'm going in there. You forget that I was a Marine. Not only that, but I was Military Police. I'll hobble a lot on my cane and look unsteady and they'll think I'm no threat."

"No!"

"There is only one man with a gun."

"The other man may have a gun."

"Trust me, Julie. I won't take any unnecessary chances. I don't want to go back into the hospital. If I caused someone to get hurt, it would be on my conscience, and I don't want that, either."

"Peter," begged Julie, but he turned to Bobby.

"Bobby, after I've been in the house three minutes, I want you to put both Sidney and Higgins in the back door. Got it?"

"Three minutes from when you step through the front door. Got it."

"Good." Peter hit his shoulder in approval. "Julie, you go with him and help manage the dogs."

"Peter."

"Go on now and get in position."

Bobby already had a hold of Higgins, and Julie reluctantly went to take Sidney's collar in her hand.

"Be careful," she admonished and followed Bobby out the back door of the barn.

Peter walked in the front door as if he suspected nothing.

"I didn't find them, Dad," he called. "Have we got company?"

"Yes," said Jacob Jones. "I'd say you have company."

Peter stopped in the doorway to the living room and surveyed the scene. Little had changed since he'd looked in an hour before.

Lisa sat on the couch next to John. The man with the gun stood near the front window. A second man stood beside the chair where his father sat, and Jacob Jones sat in his father's favorite chair. Peter carefully kept his poker face, but he was glad that Julie's uncle was in that chair. The springs were gone out of the seat and even his athletic father had to struggle to get out. Jacob would not jump into the fray when it began. The man next to his father was in a favorable position for their side as well. Peter had no doubt that his father, who had on more than one occasion subdued drunken cowhands, could deal with that character. The man would not expect a senior citizen to be as spry as his dad.

That left the man with the gun for Peter.

Peter decided that when he made his move, he would thrust the gun toward the bookcase on the opposite side of the room. If it went off by mistake, no person would be in the path of a stray bullet.

He hobbled in a few steps, leaning heavily on the cane, and he saw his father's eyes widen slightly at the sight of his unsteady progress.

"What is the meaning of this?" Peter said, eyeing the gun. "Who are you people?"

"You haven't guessed?" asked Julie's uncle. "I've come to retrieve something that belongs to me. First, I'll collect my unfortunate niece and then, in due time, the property that is mine, erroneously placed in her hands."

Peter moved awkwardly into a position that put him directly in the line of fire between his family and the gun.

"I don't think you have a realistic grasp of this situation." Peter spoke directly to Jacob Jones, seemingly unaware of the man with a gun at his back. "The courts have proven French's operation was fraudulent. No one will believe that Julie is insane."

"A woman who shoots her family and then turns the gun on herself is hardly sane, Mr. Hudson." Jacob Jones's twisted smile almost caused Peter to lose his concentration.

Peter took a step back as if recoiling in horror. From the deep recesses of the house came a howl. There was a scrabbling noise on the tiled floor of the hall, and two furry cannonballs exploded into the room. At the same moment, Peter body-slammed the rugged individual behind him, being careful to lock on to the arm holding the pistol, guiding it away from the people. Peter easily secured the gun after he had the man on the floor; he looked up to find his dad had a headlock on the other man and John was towering over Jacob Jones. Lisa sat where she had been, both dogs in her lap.

"Lisa," Peter ordered, "go tell Julie and Bobby the mission is accomplished."

"Still want to take those therapy courses?" asked Peter.

Julie looked away from the dust kicked up by the departing police cars.

"To tell you the truth, Peter, I hadn't thought much about it today."

"The reason I ask is that I'm feeling pretty full of myself right now. I subdued a hardened criminal and all, you know."

"Yes, I know," contributed his wife.

"I'd say I am pretty well rehabilitated."

"And . . ."

"And, if it's all the same to you, if you don't have your heart set on starting a career . . . mind you, you can if you want and I'll stand 100 percent behind you."

"Yes . . ."

"I just thought it would be nice to put aside adventure and intrigue for now and . . ."

"And start a family?"

Peter nodded.

"I'm a jump ahead of you, Papa."

Peter searched her face.

"You aren't kidding, are you?"

Julie grinned.

About the Author

Kathleen Paul lives in Colorado Springs, where life has gotten busier and busier now that she's retired from teaching. She leads weekly writing workshops, volunteers at church and MOPS, does crafts — currently stamping — reads, reads, reads, plays with her grandson, and tries to find time to write every day. Check out her Web site at www.donitakpaul.com.

The employees of Thorndike Press hope you have enjoyed this Large Print book. All our Thorndike and Wheeler Large Print titles are designed for easy reading, and all our books are made to last. Other Thorndike Press Large Print books are available at your library, through selected bookstores, or directly from us.

For information about titles, please call:

(800) 223-1244

or visit our Web site at:

www.gale.com/thorndike
www.gale.com/wheeler

To share your comments, please write:

Publisher
Thorndike Press
295 Kennedy Memorial Drive
Waterville, ME   04901